Merry and Moody witch cozy mysteries

Bittersweet Deceit

T. Lockhaven
WITH S.T. WHITE

TWISTED KEY
p u b l i s h i n g

2021

First Printing: 2021

ISBN 978-1-63911-004-9

Twisted Key Publishing, LLC
www.twistedkeypublishing.com

Ordering Information:
Special discounts are available on quantity purchases by corporations, associations, educators, and others. For details, contact the publisher at the above listed address.

U.S. trade bookstores and wholesalers: Please contact Twisted Key Publishing, LLC by email twistedkeypublishing@gmail.com.

Contents

1 – Raven

The raven cast its shadow over the rolling fields leading into the enchanted forest of Ashen. With a throaty caw, the majestic avian tilted its wings and dipped into the dense trees, its keen eyes focused on a trail of luminescent mushrooms that lit up the dark forest floor. Trees and vegetation flashed by as the raven's powerful wings beat a steady rhythm. Moments later, it burst from the shadows of the woodland into an open grove that led to a lonely old cottage, nestled into the hillside, tucked away from the morning sun. A lonely ranger veiled in a cloak stood on the stoop of the abandoned home. The silhouetted figure's eyes traversed the sky, and then raised its arm, granting a perfect place for the raven to perch.

"Welcome back, Brainard. I'm curious my friend," the woman spoke softly, "what did you see?"

"Coast is clear, Meryl," squawked Brainard. He fluttered his wings and adjusted his stance on his master's arm.

"Good," Meryl replied. She affectionately scratched his head. She lifted her hood which had fallen over her forehead, revealing violet eyes and hair so black it shimmered in the sunlight. "This," she gestured to the quaint cottage, "is the place Magdalyn Proctor called home."

Brainard tilted his head and ruffled his feathers. "Danger," he rasped. "Danger. Caw."

Meryl nodded and breathed out slowly. "I sense it too. Keep your eyes peeled," she said as she reached out and pressed her palm against the cool, wooden door.

The door began to vibrate and then swung open, the large metal hinges screeching the entire way. Meryl paused in the doorway; a rush of stale air greeted her. She took a measured step, placing her boot ever so carefully inside. The loose flooring groaned nosily under the weight of her step. She hesitated, her eyes explored the room, everything seemed to be the way the former sombre witch had left it. Brainard twitched nervously on Meryl's arm before fluttering up onto the rafters as she followed him. Even though she knew the house was empty, it felt like an ominous presence still lingered within. She spotted an old cauldron and a table full of empty bottles, many fallen over or shattered on the floor.

"Ransacked, ransacked," squawked Brainard from his perch.

"But the trial wasn't even a week ago," Meryl muttered. "This place has been picked clean." A loud lightheartedly. "Go back to Samuel, I'm sure he misses you over there."

Samuel poked his little white furry head from beneath the covers of Gwynevere's bed. The rat familiar twitched his nose and gave a defiant squeak, before burrowing back under the blankets. "Something tells me that's a *no*," she smirked.

Evelyn sighed and leaned on her. "You really are cold though," she said. "What's it like?"

Gwynevere looked at her and shrugged. "I'm not sure I know how to answer that, I've always been like this so…."

"Yeah, makes sense, I never really thought of it that way," Evelyn nodded.

"And other than these," she chomped her teeth together, revealing her razor-sharp fangs, "I'm no different than you."

"I'm curious, if you bit me, would I become a vampire? No, right? Because Mom was a witch, not a vampire."

Gwynevere looked at her sister and laughed. "Why would I bite you?" she asked. "And no, you wouldn't turn into a vampire, it would just hurt really, really bad. Plus, you probably taste awful."

"Hey, take that back," said Evelyn indignantly.

There was a soft knock at the bedroom door, and then the voice of Thomas Moody, Evelyn's father. "Girls, are you up?" He didn't wait for a response.

"That friendly undead woman from the city council brought breakfast."

"We're up, Dad!" shouted Evelyn. "We'll be right there." She turned to her Gwynevere, who was already halfway across the room. "It still amuses me that my dad can use the words friendly and undead in a sentence as if it's a good thing."

"I guess," shrugged Gwynevere. "I hope Dolly made blood yoke quiche. It's delicious." She rolled her eyes and steadied herself against the frame of the doorway as if she were about to faint.

Evelyn wrinkled her nose at the thought of such a thing. Samuel hopped off the bed with equal excitement, scurrying out the door behind Gwynevere. Evelyn sighed and smiled softly, soaking in the moment. For so long, it had just been her and her father, now she no longer had to wake up alone, she had a sister.

She slipped from beneath the covers into a pair of slippers and padded across the room. From the doorway, she could see her father helping Dolly, the undead maiden, fill their table with a small feast.

"Oh, wow," she muttered with wide eyes. "She really did bring us a whole breakfast."

"It smells incredible," said Gwynevere. She circled the table placing plates and silverware in front of each chair. Samuel's eyes glazed over. He swayed precariously on Gwynevere's shoulder, hypnotized by the delectable aroma of all the food. "Easy fella," she laughed, scratching behind his ears.

Evelyn rubbed her eyes and attempted to finger brush her bed head. "Good morning everyone," she yawned.

"And a good morning to you, Miss Moody," Dolly chirped with a gleeful grin. "A pleasure to see you and your family adjusting well to your new home."

Gwynevere looked at the ghoul and smiled, her keen eyes noticing that Dolly took the time to straighten her yarn-like red hair and clip it back with a beaded flower clip. Thomas had even combed his hair. He hummed happily as he pulled the chairs out for everyone.

"Freshly baked bread, corn hash, black pudding, fresh milk, red… quiche?" said Thomas as he named off everything on the table. "This is… a very kind gesture, Miss uh…."

"West," said Dolly as she squeezed her hands together and stood patiently for him to try it. "My name in life was Dorothy Alistair, but you can just call me Dolly, dear. Everyone does."

"Thank you so much, Dolly," Thomas shook his head still overwhelmed by her kindness. "You've already provided us with such a nice place to stay, and now all of this," he gestured at the small table, barely able to contain all the food. "I don't know how to thank you."

"No need to thank me, Mr. Moody, it's my duty after all," she tilted her head ever so slightly and curtsied. She turned and smiled affectionately at the girls, then made her way toward the door. "I must return to work now. Please enjoy."

"Thank you, Dolly," beamed Gwynevere. "You're the absolute best."

"Yes, thank you," smiled Evelyn.

Thomas pushed away from the table. "Dolly… are you sure you don't want to stay and enjoy this with us?"

Dolly stood at the threshold and paused. A sad smile spread across her face, she felt moved by such a kind gesture. "Thank you, sir, but I simply cannot." Her voice seemed fragile yet heavy. "I only wish to serve your needs, Merry and Moody family."

She quickly turned and closed the door behind her, leaving Thomas standing in awkward silence at the table. He turned and looked at the girls, his face filled with confusion. "Was it something I said?" he asked.

"No, the mayor keeps Dolly really busy. Too busy in my opinion. And," explained Gwynevere, "since she is a ghoul, she doesn't need to eat or drink."

"Oh," said Thomas, sliding back into his chair. He eyed the table filled with food. It had been a long time since he had been able to provide Evelyn with such a meal. "Of course," he said softly, "I should've known that."

Gwynevere smiled kindly at him, "You're doing great."

Rufus padded lazily into the kitchen, announcing his presence with a series of meows. He brushed his body against Evelyn's legs and then plopped to the ground at her feet.

"Good morning, Rufus." She grabbed a small plate and filled it with black pudding and eggs for her familiar. He thanked her with a heavy dose of purring as he dug right in.

Samuel pulled at Gwynevere's silvery white hair, squeaking uncontrollably. "Okay, okay," she sighed. "A little patience." She slid a tiny plate beside her own and filled it with egg and corn hash. Samuel scurried down her arm, squeaking excitedly as she placed the plate on the floor.

For quite some time, the only sound was the scraping of forks on plates. Gwynevere watched her new family enjoying their meal. She was well aware that both Thomas and Evelyn had a lot to learn about life in Ashen. It had only been three days since they moved into Dolly's unoccupied home after the trial of Gwynevere's grandmother, Mama Maggie. Thomas seemed distant. His mind was clearly elsewhere, even as the family was coming together for their first real meal in days.

"It sure beats bread and soup?" smiled Gwynevere between bites, trying to bring life back to the table.

"Yes. Yes. Where are my manners?" Thomas exclaimed. "I'm sorry, Gwynevere, I got lost in my own head for a moment."

"It's okay," Gwynevere smiled affectionately at him. "It's a lot to take in. Give it some time."

"I had another nightmare by the way," said Evelyn as she began sampling the quiche.

"I know," said Thomas. He took a sip from his glass of milk and pointed to a picture hanging cockeyed on the wall. "It felt like an earthquake."

Gwynevere looked at the two of them and sat her fork down. "Mr. Moody, do you think it would be okay if I took Evelyn into the city today? You know, to do a little exploring."

Evelyn's eyes slid from Gwynevere to her father, he wasn't big on exploring. He wiped his mouth with a napkin, wriggled his nose and nodded. "Well… I think Evelyn is old enough to make her own decisions on the matter." He smiled at Evelyn, in a way he hadn't in years. It was as if her father was finding himself again. "The last thing I want you to do is coop yourself inside the house because of me."

"I know," said Evelyn. "It's just that things are so different here. I have to admit, I'm a little scared of going out there."

"I understand," nodded Gwynevere, "however, we have to face our fears. We can't just keep sitting here waiting for the Academy to come talk to us again. It was unheard-of for Headmaster Ozark to approach us like he did. That is a rare opportunity. It's not every day you get invited to the Academy for tea." She tilted her head and met Evelyn's eyes.

"They said they'd be in contact with us when they learned something new about our mother's case."

"So, you would rather sit here? Opportunity has already knocked, I'm not confident that it's going to knock twice."

"It has been a while," Evelyn agreed.

"Almost a week," Gwynevere replied. "Too long in my opinion."

"Too long!" squawked the shrill voice of a raven as it alighted onto a rafter above the table.

Both Evelyn and Gwynevere jumped in their seats. Thomas flung his fork across the kitchen and shot backward in his chair. "Where did that bird come from?!" he gasped.

Rufus looked up at the familiar and hissed. The raven tilted his head and fluttered his wings. Samuel raced up Gwynevere's leg to her lap, squeaking the entire way. "Oh," said Gwynevere. "The Academy?" Samuel nodded.

She jumped up from the table. "Evelyn! They're summoning us to the Academy!"

"We're being summoned by a crow?" asked Evelyn.

"Raven. Caw. I'm a raven."

"I believe you've offended our guest," said Gwynevere.

"My humblest apologies." Evelyn turned to her father. "I know it's unusual, being summoned by," she gestured toward the raven, "a bird, but is it okay if I go, Father?"

Thomas wiped his mouth and chuckled. "Yes, yes, go," he waved her on.

Evelyn reached across the table, snatched up a piece of bread and stuffed it in her mouth. Gwynevere had already bolted from the table. There was a screech from the kitchen, and then the hurried sound of slippers racing down the hallway. Evelyn slammed the bedroom door, leaving Thomas alone at the table with the three familiars. He glanced at Rufus and Samuel who seemed to be staring him down. "So," he cleared his throat. "A friend of yours?" he asked, feeling a little silly talking to a rat.

Samuel twitched his whiskers and puffed out his furry chest as both girls burst out of the bedroom. "Bye, Dad," Evelyn waved with a smile.

"Bye, Mr. Moody," said Gwynevere with a tilt of her mother's pointy hat. She paused for a moment as Samuel leapt off the table, slid across the floor, then scrambled up her leg, over her dress and into her hat.

Thomas whirled in his seat. "That was fast," he said, trying to comprehend how they had changed their clothes so quickly. "Were you wearing your clothes beneath your night gowns?"

"A proper witch must always be ready at the blink of an eye," said Gwynevere with a playful wink. She pushed the door open and glanced up at the raven. "Come on!"

Evelyn who was already waiting on the front stoop, turned into the doorway and patted her thighs. Rufus meowed and yawned, letting out one more good stretch before padding across the room and leaping into Evelyn's arms. She smiled; her heart was filled with excitement. She was nervous, but excited to embrace the new city, and a new adventure. She locked hands with her sister as they followed the mysterious raven through the bustling streets of Ashen to their destination, the prestigious Ashen Academy.

2 - Remnant

"It's like a fortress," said Evelyn, her voice filled with wonderment. Gwynevere nodded as the massive iron gates to the Academy slowly opened like two giant arms welcoming them. The two sisters passed beneath a great stone archway following a cobblestone pathway that led them through a sprawling line of trees. Golden rays peeked through the canopy of trees dappling the forest floor with splotches of sunlight. Samuel poked his bewhiskered nose from the rim of Gwynevere's hat and squeaked at a luminescent butterfly who had alighted there. The butterfly sat for a moment, then fluttered away.

"Oh yes, thank you for the protection, Samuel." The rat squeaked again. "Yes, I wouldn't have wanted to be carried away… by a butterfly."

Evelyn covered her mouth and laughed behind her hand. Rufus tapped Evelyn's chest with a furry paw and meowed. "Of course, you can get down." Rufus leapt from her arms and immediately began chasing butterflies. "He didn't want to feel left out since you were doling out compliments," Evelyn laughed.

"I am half-blood, just as you are human and witch, I am elf and magus."

Brainard flapped his wings and cawed. Meryl stroked the bird's feathers and nodded. "You're right, my friend." She turned her attention back to the girls. "Come, come. The headmaster is waiting."

Gwynevere took Evelyn's hand in hers, "Together?"

"Together," laughed Evelyn with a quick nod.

With a wave of her hand, the giant doors leading into the rib vault hall opened. The interior was cool. Dazzling rays of colorful sunlight shone through massive stained-glass windows creating a rainbow of colors on the white marble floors. The sound of their footsteps echoed as they passed fantastical artwork in ornate golden frames and armor dating back many centuries. Evelyn eyed a tapestry that depicted a young man surrounded by amazed onlookers as he pulled a sword from a stone. She stopped for a moment to stare.

"I see one of the tapestries has caught your attention." Meryl positioned herself beside Evelyn. "These tapestries tell many tales of our world's history. Generation after generation has used this unique form of storytelling to pass on our history, from inception to as recent as the turn of the century."

"This story, my father used to tell me about King Arthur, and the sword in the stone. Is there a lot of crossover between this world's history and the mortal world?" Evelyn asked.

Meryl's expression turned somber. She raised her arm and Brainard fluttered into the air, landing on a nearby suit of armor. "Yes, more than any art or historical text can depict." She thought for a moment, then smiled tightly, "Come, follow me to the library."

"The library, or *the* library?" asked Gwynevere. "Miss Ambrosius," Gwynevere gasped, straightening her hat, "are we about to be initiated into the Academy?"

There was no answer from Meryl, just the steady *whisk, whisk* of her cloak, and she walked ahead briskly.

Evelyn blinked, confused. "Gwynevere." She grabbed her sister by the sleeve. "What do you mean be initiated? What's happening?"

"The Academy Library is famous. It contains the largest archive of magical knowledge in the world," whispered Gwynevere. "Trust me, they don't just let anyone go in there."

"Oh…," replied Evelyn. "I still don't understand what this means."

Meryl spun on her heels and faced the girls. "Yes. What Gwynevere says about the library's collection of magical artifacts and resources is true. It is unparalleled. There is no equal in existence. As far as the headmaster's intentions, it is not my place to assume. I only know that he has requested this meeting for a very specific reason."

"I should have brought my broom," whispered Gwynevere to Evelyn as they turned another corner in the complex maze of hallways. Meryl came to a stop in front of a plain wooden door, with an underwhelming gold placard with the word 'Library' engraved into it. A wave of doubt passed through Gwynevere as she stared at the simple door. *Maybe I was wrong. Surely, the famous library would have a spectacular entrance.*

Meryl waved her hand, and the door swung open, revealing a room that took not only Gwynevere's doubts away, but her breath. Samuel curiously popped his head out from under her hat. Evelyn stepped through the doorway; her eyes ping-ponged around the room. She had never seen so many books. There were multiple stories filled with bookshelves, towering cases of magical implements, and in the center of the room, standing behind a lectern, was the tall and stoic Headmaster Ozark.

He looked up at the girls and smiled behind a huge furry mustache that nearly covered up his entire face. His eyes danced behind thick-rimmed glasses. He wore a purple cape that billowed and moved about as if it had a life of its own. He motioned the group over and then returned his attention to an open-faced book sitting atop the lectern. A charred piece of wood bearing a strange runic symbol, lay between the pages.

"Welcome, Merry and Moody sisters," his voice was deep and rich. "You're just in time."

"Morning, Headmaster," the sisters chorused and curtsied.

As the girls approached, the blood droplet rune began to pulsate, causing the small piece of wood to quiver, thus making the book shake as well. The headmaster turned to the girls with piqued interest.

"Where did you find that?!" gasped Gwynevere, eyeing the magical artifact. "That looks like my father's!"

Meryl looked at the young witch and raised a brow. "You can recognize a piece of wood?" she asked.

"No ma'am," said Gwynevere politely. "I recognize the symbol. It's the symbol of my father's bloodline."

The headmaster loomed over her and sighed. "I was afraid you would say that."

"I… I'm confused," Gwynevere looked from the headmaster to Meryl. "Is something wrong?" she asked slowly.

"My dear, do you understand what a *remnant* is?" asked Meryl.

"No," said Gwynevere uncertainly, "should I?"

"I know what it is," Evelyn felt her cheeks grow red as the headmaster and Meryl turned their attention to her. She cleared her throat and continued, "A remnant is a magical artifact imbued with the memories of its bearer. Oftentimes, they are used to preserve memories of loved ones."

A pleased expression filled the headmaster's face. He rubbed a hand across his wooly mustache. "Interesting, and how do you know that?"

"My mother gave me a book that covered the history of magic, each page was filled with her notes and observations and even recipes," said Evelyn with a half-smile, "and I devoured all of it. I remembered reading about remnants because I often lingered on the idea of such things being real." She looked at her sister, "I was hoping I would find something of hers, you know, to remember her by," she squeezed Gwynevere's hand, "and yet I found something even more special."

"I had no idea," said Gwynevere, feeling embarrassed.

"Don't be so hard on yourself, Ms. Merry," insisted the headmaster. "You're young and you still have a lot to learn. Both of you." His tone was soft and reassuring.

"Yes sir," said Gwynevere sheepishly.

"Is that what you wanted to show us?" asked Evelyn. "The remnant?"

"I was hoping for Merry's insight, since she confirmed the symbol is directly affiliated to the house of her father's bloodline. But," added the headmaster kindly, "you should feel no shame, as I said, you have much to learn."

"I can see that," said Gwynevere. "It's just that my father chose to never share much about his family. They were always a mystery to me. I'm sorry I wasn't much help."

The headmaster glanced at the piece of wood and rubbed his finger along the ruin. He turned and looked down at the young dhampir thoughtfully. "Maybe there is a way you can help. The remnant did react strongly to your presence."

"Really?!" Hope rekindled inside of her.

The headmaster motioned for her to join him behind the lectern. "Would you mind holding the remnant? Perhaps you will be able to see things Miss Ambrosius could not."

Gwynevere nodded excitedly. "I doubt I will be able to see anything Miss Ambrosius couldn't see, but I'll try."

Her fingers were just about to touch the scarred piece of wood when Meryl added, "I would advise handling it with care."

"Caw! Handle with care!" warned Brainard, flapping his wings.

"Jeesh." Gwynevere stole a nervous glance at the two grown-ups and then to her sister, who gave her a smile of encouragement. Before her fingers had a chance to completely encircle the remnant, powerful magic pulsed through her—suddenly everything turned black and everyone vanished. She was no longer in the library or within the walls of the Academy. She was at her old home, with her father.

"Dad?" she gasped and stared into his eyes, confused. He returned her gaze, smiling softly. He was tall, dark and regal, just as Gwynevere remembered. "Dad, is it really you?" She desperately wanted her vision to be true. This moment, this moment in time, she remembered it well. It was the last time she'd spoken to her father. He reached into his pocket and removed a golden-clasped watch. He deftly opened it with his finger and then, as if they were on a stroll through the park, casually checked the time.

He cast a curious glance toward Gwynevere. "My dear, have I ever told you about the Sanguines Drop?"

"No, Father," she balled up her face, this was all so confusing. "You never told me."

His face softened, "And now, my dear, people have come to you seeking answers to questions you can't even begin to answer." He watched her intently. Gwynevere began to shake. Was this really happening or was it a memory recorded in the remnant? How did it all work?

She slowly reached out to touch him, to confirm that he was truly there, only to see her hand pass through him and reveal the illusion. Her eyes began to water, she tilted her gaze downward as she struggled to stay strong in his presence. "The Sanguines Drop is a vessel of ancient making, said to preserve the blood of a treasured loved one."

"Yes, Father," she whispered, "often used in vampire rituals of resurrection. I read the letter," she explained.

Adonis knelt beside his daughter. "Listen to me, never let them have it, my dear. It is entrusted to you, and only you." He held her stare, willing her to understand. "Others will try to take it from you." A sadness filled his eyes, "Your mother and I will not be there to protect you, but that doesn't mean that you won't be protected. Follow your blood, my sweet dhampir."

Tears ran down Gwynevere's cheeks, "Father," she cried, "I don't understand. Why did you and mother have to go? Why did you leave me? I don't even know where the Sanguines Drop is or how to find it."

The illusion of Adonis began to flicker. He was fading away.

"Dad, I need answers, please! Please don't go! How can I protect something if I don't know where... it is?" Her voice gave way to sobs, it was as if she was losing her father all over again. In his final lingering moments, he reached inside his cloak and removed a familiar piece of wood. He bared his fangs and breathed on it, creating the runic symbol and imprinting the memory. Then, he was nothing more than a million shimmering particles swirling before her.

"Gwynevere." A voice pulled at her, swimming around in her head. "Gwynevere." She felt a hand grab her shoulder and she wrapped herself up in Evelyn's arms, sobbing.

"It's okay! I'm here," Evelyn whispered. Samuel scurried from beneath Gwynevere's hat, crawled down to her shoulder and gently nuzzled his whiskery nose against her cheek.

Meryl crossed her arms and curiously eyed the headmaster, who studied the girls in silence. "Please understand, Headmaster, that I say this with the *utmost* respect," Meryl whispered. "But I'm not sure if it's wise to continue involving these children in the investigations." She paused, attempting to get a read on the headmaster's thoughts, but he remained stone-faced. "I simply believe that the Academy should focus on their education and helping them move on from this tragedy, not dwell on it."

"No. I appreciate your concern. However, the girls are already immersed in this mess. Mitigation of their involvement is not what's needed."

"I see," said Meryl. "So what would you have me do, Headmaster?"

"Continue with your investigation."

"And as for Gwynevere?"

"I believe that it is Ms. Merry's decision as to how she proceeds with the information divulged to her." He stroked his mustache and gazed up at the domed ceiling. "Keep a close eye on the girls. Assist as needed. I suspect things are about to get… interesting."

"I'll do everything I can to help them," said Meryl solemnly.

"I know you will. I don't have to tell you that the mayor sent his best investigators to Proctor's home, and they were unable to figure out who the woman was that you found or why she was there. From your vision, we know she was burning pages from a book."

"Yes, and then brutally murdered," said Meryl.

"I have my suspicions, but I'll wait to see what your investigation reveals. I don't want to say too much, I'd prefer to let your instincts guide you."

Brainard swooped overhead releasing a raspy caw that echoed off the buildings. Meryl cocked an annoyed eyebrow at the raven.

"That confounded bird," Headmaster Ozark shook his head. "For now, focus on identifying the woman and figuring out what she was burning. I fear that it has something to do with the magical artifacts that were stolen from the Academy."

"You think Magdalyn Proctor was hiding the stolen artifacts in her home?"

"I do, and if this is true, then whatever she was hiding in that secret room, is now in the hands of our enemies. The one thing we must protect," Meryl followed his gaze, "is young Merry. She holds the key to the most valuable artifact ever created…."

"The Sanguines Drop," said Meryl, finishing his sentence.

"Yes. It is my intention to have them initiated into the Academy as soon as this unfortunate incident is resolved." With those words, Headmaster Ozark spun on his heel, and disappeared back into the library.

Meryl rejoined the two sisters, the confusion and frustration on Gwynevere's face was palatable. She had been asked to protect something that she didn't physically possess. Not only that, she had no idea where to find this powerful magical relic. Why did her father have to talk to her in riddles?

Meryl seemed to be able to sense what she was thinking. "I, too, saw a vision when I held the relic, and just like you, I am confused by what I saw… by what was revealed to me."

"I saw my father, he told me that there was something I must protect… but what he's asking is impossible. It's as if he told me to protect a ghost… it only exists in my imagination. Do you understand?" asked Gwynevere.

"I do," Meryl spoke softly. "But in my hundreds of years of practicing magic, I've learned that time provides answers."

"That's so—"

Meryl held up a finger silencing Gwynevere. "I'm not talking about the mere passage of time, I'm speaking of progression, continuation—the idea that we will unconsciously and consciously move toward the answer."

"That actually makes sense," said Evelyn. "It's sort of like our *will* knows that we need the answer, so our subconscious mind continues to work on the solution."

"Precisely!" exclaimed Meryl. "Don't you worry, young Merry, the answer will come to you, just as the answer to my vision will divulge itself to me as well."

Gwynevere nodded, she felt as if the tremendous weight that was resting on her shoulders was slowly melting away. "Thank you," she whispered.

"You're welcome. Now, follow me," said Meryl gently. "I know you have a lot on your mind. Let me show you where I like to go when I need to clear my thoughts."

Evelyn nodded and grabbed her sister's hand. She gave it a gentle squeeze as they followed Meryl into the sparkling sunlight.

3 – Academy

Brainard circled high above the courtyard keeping a watchful eye on his master. His shrill caws filled the air.

"I can never tell if he's warning us of some great danger, or if he's just talking," said Gwynevere, watching the raven cut across the sky, following the invisible currents.

At that moment, Evelyn could have cared less about the bird. She stood in awe of the vast courtyard that sat at the center of the Academy. "Gwynevere, look at the perfectly manicured trees, and those flowers, I love how they frame the castle. It's absolutely breathtaking."

Gwynevere looked at her sister and cocked an eyebrow, it was difficult to remain in the doldrums when Evelyn was so excited. "Are you okay? It's just a castle."

Evelyn waved Gwynevere's comment aside. "Look at this place, the architecture, the symmetry. So much symmetry. Honestly, I've only seen its likeness in books. I feel like we're living in one of those romantic poems by Lord Byron."

Meryl couldn't help but laugh at Evelyn's enthusiasm. "You're well-read for a child that grew up in the human world. You share your mother's taste and sophistication."

"Thank you, but it really wasn't the human world. It was a magical fabrication, just made to resemble it," explained Evelyn.

"I'm aware," replied Meryl, shaking her head. "Ah, but where are my manners? Please understand, I didn't mean to appear insensitive to your… case. You were forced to live in near poverty for many years, and the fact that you learned to read so young is admirable."

"My father taught me." Evelyn's thoughts disappeared to her sitting at the counter in their shop. Mr. Moody teaching her the alphabet and simple words. "He had a lot of patience," Evelyn smiled.

Samuel climbed down to Gwynevere's shoulder and squeaked loudly. "I'm not sure, I'll ask," replied the young witch. "I'm curious, Miss Ambrosius, why did you bring us here?" Samuel nodded his approval and twitched his whiskers.

"Please, call me Meryl," the elf insisted. "You were brought here because Headmaster Ozark believes it imperative that you receive academic lessons that will help accelerate your initiation process into the Academy." She tilted her head, "It wasn't by happenstance that he chose me to be your mentor, mind you."

"Thank you," said Evelyn respectfully. "But where are all the students?"

"I was wondering the same thing," added Gwynevere.

"No need to worry about them. For now, I will need your utmost attention without distractions—"

"Did he send all the students home?" Gwynevere took in the empty courtyard. "The headmaster wants you to train us for something big, doesn't he?" Samuel stood on his hind legs and squeaked his agreement. "Samuel said he overheard what the headmaster said before he left." Samuel cast a worried look at Meryl, who was now staring at him. His furry throat gulped, and he disappeared beneath Gwynevere's hat.

Evelyn shook her head and looked at Meryl. "Is that true?"

An exasperated sigh escaped Meryl's lips. "Of course, it's true. Gwynevere dear, you should know better than anyone that the worst can happen when you least expect it. It is my responsibility to make sure you girls know how to handle your abilities. Especially you, Evelyn."

Evelyn half-smiled and nodded. "I'm a fast learner, Miss Ambrosius."

"And modest," whispered Gwynevere.

"I'm sure you are. Now, enough of the chit-chat," said Meryl, rubbing her hands together. "I need to get a measure of your skill level. What do you girls know in the way of the arcane arts?"

Samuel parted Gwynevere's hair and peeked out. Things were getting interesting. "My mom taught me mostly alchemical spells." She rubbed her chin thoughtfully. "However, I do know a few tricks," her ruby eyes sparkled mischievously.

"Wait," said Evelyn, "what was the spell you used to help us escape from the werewolf?"

"Oh yes, of course," nodded Gwynevere. "That's a good one!"

Meryl narrowed her eyes and crossed her arms. "You escaped a werewolf?" Gwynevere could tell by her teacher's voice she was impressed. "Alright, let's see."

Everyone, including Samuel, jumped when Gwynevere slapped her hands together and shouted "Explodiamo!" A powerful burst of smoke billowed in a swirling ball in front of her. Meryl blinked and did her best not to laugh. She coughed politely into her hand to hide her smile. Gwynevere looked at her and wrinkled her nose. "What's so funny?"

"I'm curious, why did you shout *Explodiamo*?" she chuckled.

Gwynevere blinked and flicked her fangs. She turned to Evelyn and then to Samuel for some type of affirmation. "Aren't we supposed to say the name of the spells?" she asked.

"No, my dear," Meryl chuckled, "that's just silly. Who told you that?"

Gwynevere's cheeks brightened, matching her red eyes. "My father. He said magic is emboldened when spoken with passion and vigor."

"I see." Meryl cupped her chin in her hand. "I'm sorry to tell you this, but your father was merely pulling your leg."

"No! My father was not a puller of legs, I assure you," said Gwynevere earnestly.

Meryl smiled and her violet eyes began to glow. "Observe, my child." She held out her hand and lightly wriggled her fingers. A swirling ball of light hovered above her palms. She breathed in deeply, the ball of light responded, growing brighter, pulsating as it drew in energy from the air within the courtyard.

Gwynevere and Evelyn raised their hands to their faces, protecting their eyes as the magical power rippled in waves around them. There was a bright flash and then an ear-shattering explosion of heat and smoke. Gwynevere felt the impact like a punch to the chest.

"Woah," gasped Gwynevere in awe as she righted her hat. "That was amazing!" Samuel squeaked excitedly from beneath her hat. "Samuel says woah, too."

Brainard swooped from the sky and lit upon Meryl's outstretched arm. He fluttered his wings and squawked. "Caw! Watch and learn!"

"That was beautiful," cried Evelyn, hardly able to contain her excitement, "can you do that again?"

Meryl gave the girls a crooked grin. "Magic is beautiful but also very dangerous. One must learn incredible focus to achieve great things. I'm afraid you cannot do that by shouting made-up words."

Gwynevere looked down at her feet and blushed. "I'm sorry, I didn't realize my father had been teasing me."

Meryl placed her hand on the young dhampir's shoulder. "There's no need to be sorry. We must all start somewhere, and it's important that you have a great teacher." She gave Gwynevere a wink. "You know, you remind me a lot of myself when I was your age. You both do," she said turning to Evelyn.

"Really?" asked Evelyn.

"Yes," Meryl nodded reassuringly. "Now, listen closely. There are two forms of defensive magic suitable for young witches of your caliber."

"Caw," cried Brainard flapping his wings. "*Luxations* and conjuration *minoras*.

"Luxations?" asked Evelyn curiously.

"Yes, the powerful spell you just witnessed harnesses the power of light. It is known as a luxation majoras," explained Meryl. "The reason you need guidance and focus is, this type of magic is extremely volatile. Had I not been able to contain the explosion, we would have all been visiting the infirmary. I think our first lesson will be manipulating fire."

"I know how to manipulate fire," said Evelyn. "Well, nothing close to your abilities," she quickly added.

"I do, too," said Gwynevere.

Meryl crossed her arms and studied the girls closely. "I guess I'm not surprised. You were both born of powerful witch blood. I'm sure that a lot of this will come naturally through the art of conflagration—which I am not permitted to teach until you are at least sophomore initiates in the Academy."

"So, fire magic is illegal?" asked Gwynevere.

"Not illegal, more so ill-advised," explained Meryl. "But," she gave the girls a crafty grin, "being your teacher, I suppose that it would be prudent that I ascertain your magical abilities."

"Oh!" Gwynevere clapped her hands excitedly. "Fire is my favorite."

"I may regret this," said Meryl, shaking her head. "Indulge me." She waved her hand, creating a line of four floating candles.

Gwynevere and Evelyn both opened their mouths in awe at how easily their mentor conjured such objects.

"Don't be too impressed. This type of magic is used to create simple objects, such as a candle. However, objects created through this type of magic, conjuration minoras will only remain as long as the conjurer remains focused on their existence. It takes an exceptional mind to manifest objects of a more—" Meryl's eyes widened. Without so much as a blink, Evelyn had created a candle sitting on a brass pricket. Unattended, Meryl's candles fell to the ground and vanished.

Evelyn smiled bashfully as Gwynevere lightly touched the wick, setting it alight. She smiled at her sister with the biggest proudest grin she could muster, giving a rare glimpse at her sharp little vampire teeth.

"I don't think you'll have a problem with either of us keeping up, Miss Ambrosius," smiled Gwynevere.

Meryl looked at the both of them and sighed before laughing. "Oh, Adelaide, they remind me so much of you in so many ways," she said to herself. "Very well, dears, I won't linger too much on the wordy details."

"Sorry, Miss Ambrosius," said Evelyn. "I wasn't trying to be disrespectful."

Meryl reached out and placed a hand on each of the girl's arms. "You two have nothing to worry about. Trust me." She watched as Evelyn and Gwynevere broke into smiles. Though they had innate talent, shc knew that they were both still young and very impressionable, especially in the situation they found themselves in. She sighed heavily. "And for the last time, I swear by my ancestor's beard, just call me Meryl."

4 – Invitation

It was dusk when the sisters left the Academy. Meryl and Brainard had sent them off with buzzing heads filled with new magical knowledge. Evelyn reunited with Rufus, who was napping on a tree stump. He'd exhausted himself hunting and most likely—from the telltale glowing whiskers—eaten a few luminous butterflies.

"Silly cat," laughed Evelyn, "I suppose you're just about done for the day." She picked up her lazy cat and cradled him in her arms. Rufus snuggled in and meowed.

"Yes," Evelyn replied. "It was exquisite. I learned so much, and our mentor is a *direct* descendant of the great wizard *Merlin*." Rufus twitched his ears and gave Evelyn a dubious look.

"It's true," Gwynevere affirmed. "I'm not sure if he believes you, he's giving you that look." Rufus turned to Gwynevere, and decided he was too tired to argue. "I don't know about you," she said, changing the subject, "but I'm getting kind of hungry. I hope your father saved some of the food Dolly brought us."

"There is no way he ate all that food by himself," laughed Evelyn. She drew closer to her sister as they exited the gates of the Academy and into the city. Night was settling in, and the streets and sidewalks were filled with townsfolk of all shapes and sizes. Evelyn eyed them warily. She knew she shouldn't feel uncomfortable but having grown up in the 'human' world, well, Ashen seemed so unusual. Gwynevere took notice and slid her arm through Evelyn's.

Evelyn smiled. "You caught me," she scrunched her nose. "I'm getting there, it's just a little strange being somewhere so different."

"That's because you've been shut up inside the house since you got here," Gwynevere said playfully. "Pretty soon, everything will seem normal. We'll keep learning from Miss Ambrosius, and we'll both help your father adapt to Ashen. I know it's not easy, but it's your new home."

Evelyn nodded thoughtfully. A pair of fairies flitted past, their little wings glowing brightly in beautiful hues of gold and green. "It is amazing here, so vibrant and alive."

Gwynevere beamed as they strolled down the cobblestone path to their house. She pushed open the door and strode inside. "We're home!" she announced.

Thomas peered over his reading glasses from the comfort of his rocking chair. Rufus leapt from Evelyn's arms, scampered across the living room, and effortlessly bounded onto his lap. "Well hello Rufus," Thomas chuckled. He set the newspaper aside and affectionately scratched the furry feline behind his ears. Rufus responded by pushing the back of his head against his hand and purring loudly. "I was wondering when you two were going to come home." *Home*, the word felt strange on his lips.

"Oh, Father," Evelyn gushed. She rushed over and hugged him. "The Academy is beautiful! I've never seen anything like it. It's amazing and our teacher is a direct descendant of Merlin."

"Merlin?" asked Thomas. "The wizard of folklore?" Rufus rolled his eyes and gave a *here we go again* meow.

"Yes," squeaked Evelyn, ignoring Rufus. "She's incredible!"

"I would imagine so. There's never been a more famous wizard."

Gwynevere's heart filled with warmth. It was so wonderful to see Thomas so relaxed, and the utter joy on Evelyn's face. She glanced over at the dining room table. *Yes!* It was packed with rolls and pastries. Gwynevere imagined a plate filled with delectables, until her eyes fell upon an envelope with a familiar stamp, bearing her family's crest.

"Mr. Moody," asked Gwynevere, snatching the letter off the table, "where did this come from?" She held the envelope aloft, examining the smudge of red wax which bore an imprint of her father's house seal.

"Oh, yes," said Mr. Moody, adjusting his glasses, "I forgot to tell you. It came through that slot in the door." He pointed to a large rectangular opening at the bottom of the door.

"Not where it physically came from," replied Gwynevere, "I mean did you see who delivered it?" Samuel poked his head out from under her hat, his curiosity piqued.

"Well, that's a different question altogether. I'm sorry, I didn't see who delivered it. I was reading the Ashen newspaper, which is fascinating by the way," he thumped the newspaper with his fingertips, "and when I looked up, it was laying on the floor."

"Is it from the university?" asked Evelyn.

"No," replied Gwynevere, "it has my family's stamp," her voice trailed off as she thought of her father and the vision she'd had at the school that day. The appearance of the remnant and now a letter from her family, the timing seemed very curious.

"Well open it," prompted Thomas. Rufus meowed in agreement.

"Okay," Gwynevere sighed, using her little vampire nails to cut into the wax and open the letter by hand. She unfolded the white parchment and raised an eyebrow. "It's from Elise Merry."

"Who is Elise Merry?" asked Evelyn excitedly. "What does it say?"

Gwynevere shrugged and continued reading for a moment before answering. "Oh!" she exclaimed. "Elise is Judge Aiden's sister."

"The one that was murdered?!" Evelyn exclaimed.

Gwynevere nodded, "I never realized that Judge Aiden was a Merry." She continued to read in silence as her eyes slid down the page.

"Is everything okay?" asked Evelyn, trying to read her sister's expression. "I'm sorry, but you're keeping us on pins and needles."

"First, I have absolutely no idea what that means. Second, yes, everything seems to be okay. She wants me to meet her tonight at the Merry Mansion." Evelyn's body stiffened. Such a request was a little unusual. "She says she has information that's too sensitive to divulge in a letter."

"Tonight? That's a little sudden, don't you think?" asked Mr. Moody.

Evelyn nodded, agreeing with her father. "I was thinking the same thing. You've never met this person. Don't you think it's a little odd?"

"Truthfully, I don't know most of my family," explained Gwynevere. "After my father married outside the bloodline, we were considered outcasts. There is a lot of pride in the vampiric bloodline to remain pureblood. I'm honestly surprised anyone would want to reach out to me at all." Samuel crawled down to his master's shoulder and nuzzled against her cheek.

"I see." Evelyn paced back and forth across the room. "So, she wants you to meet her at the Merry mansion." She continued pacing, and then another thought hit her. "Wait, if you have a mansion, why did Dolly have to give us her home?"

"Yes, she wants me to meet her at the Merry Mansion. No, the mansion is not mine, it's the Merry *family* mansion," she clarified. Rufus lowered his head back onto Thomas's lap, having already lost interest in the conversation. "You realize you're going to wear out the carpet if you keep pacing."

"Please continue," Evelyn insisted. "I'm deep in thought."

"Obviously…. My father said the mansion has been empty for many years. And before you ask, I have no idea why." Gwynevere's eyes dropped back to the letter. "I think I should go. It could be the perfect opportunity to ask some questions about my father and maybe she knows more about the Sanguines Drop."

Evelyn casually looked over Gwynevere's shoulder at the letter and rubbed her chin suspiciously. "Or maybe she's going to…," Evelyn's eyes flew open wide, and she made wiggly fingers at her sister.

"Tickle me?" asked Gwynevere. "What?"

"Whatever she wants… well, I don't think it's safe. Why not meet you during the day? And why the sudden urgency?"

"I agree," said Thomas. "Why not wait till morning?"

"Most of my family is on my father's side," said Gwynevere. "They're all full-blooded vampires. They do not operate during the day. Only a half-blood like me can stand sunlight. Nightly get-togethers are normal. I'm sure I'll be fine."

"Well, maybe she could help you understand what your father told you. And I have to agree, she may have some insights on the Sanguines Drop," Evelyn capitulated.

Gwynevere nodded, "Plus you'll save the carpet from all of your pacing," she teased. "But seriously, this may be an opportunity for me to connect with some of my family. If she has any information about my father's whereabouts, it would be worth it."

Thomas still looked skeptical, but he realized he needed to learn to readjust to life here in Ashen. The rules were different than in the human world.

Samuel pulled on her earlobe and squeaked with excitement. "Samuel wants you all to know that he will protect me, if I fall into any unforeseen misfortune." Her familiar stood on his hind legs and nodded in agreement. She turned to Mr. Moody, "I promise we won't be long, and I can take care of myself," said Gwynevere.

"She did Explodiamo a werewolf," Evelyn added.

"It's not too far, I hope," said Thomas. Rufus stood and rubbed his head against Thomas's chest. "I'm just concerned with you going out at night."

"Well, she is kind of half-nocturnal, Father," said Evelyn.

"I know," he sighed. "Alright, but promise me you won't linger, and you'll return straightaway without—"

"Father," Evelyn said softly. "You're doing it again."

Thomas smiled, "You're right. It's hard *not* being a father. Someday you'll understand when you're a parent."

"So I can go?" asked Gwynevere excitedly.

"Yes," Thomas smiled, "you can go."

She was planning on sneaking out the window as soon as he went to bed if he'd said no, but his agreeing to let her go was so much better.

"Oh, how I wish I could take the both of you," said Gwynevere with a lighthearted smile. "But with Thomas being a *human*, and Elise pure vampire…," she gave a devious smile, "we should probably hold off on that for now."

"Uhm, I don't mind if we hold off on the introductions indefinitely," Thomas said.

Gwynevere chuckled. She scooped Samuel from her shoulder and gently tapped his nose. "Who's up for an adventure?" Samuel squeaked robustly, which is hard to do for a rat. "Well, that settle's it."

Evelyn brushed her hair from her face and gave her sister a hug. "You won't be gone long, right?"

"I'm just going to go and see what this is about and ask a few questions," said Gwynevere.

"Well, just remember, if things get tough, don't be afraid to use your secret weapon," said Evelyn with a snicker.

Gwynevere wrinkled her nose and playfully shoved Evelyn. "You're not going to let me off the hook with that, are you?"

"Not on your life," laughed Evelyn.

Gwynevere turned her attention to Thomas. "Well then, Mr. Moody, I'll be back long before dawn. Don't wait up for me. The mansion isn't far by broom."

Thomas looked bewildered as he contemplated *when* exactly he had usurped control as their guardian. Gwynevere crossed the room and flung open the door to the closet. She stretched out her arm. There was a click-clacking sound of wood against wood, and then a meaty thwack as her broom flew out of the closet and into her hand.

Evelyn's eyes popped with excitement. "Is that Mother's?" she asked.

Gwynevere grinned and showed her sharp little teeth. "It is. I'll teach you how to ride it when I get back." She opened the front door and paused. "Only if you promise me you won't stay cooped up in this house anymore."

"I promise," said Evelyn with a mischievous twinkle in her eyes. *I'll be right behind you.*

"Good," said Gwynevere as she tipped her hat and waved goodbye to her family. "Don't worry about me. I'll be back, hopefully with some news about Mother or Father."

As soon as Gwynevere was out the door, Evelyn dove into the closet, flinging clothes and shoes into the hallway.

"What are you doing?" asked Thomas, jumping to his feet and sending Rufus flying.

"Taking care of my little sister. I'll be right back. I promise." With that, Evelyn flung the front door open, jumped on the broom and took off into the air in a single bound. The broom gained momentum and height unexpectantly fast. As she rocketed above the city, she could see her sister—she was nothing more than a tiny speck, flying away.

Far below, Thomas stood on the porch, staring up at the sky as his daughter disappeared over the tree line. "Did you know she could fly?" he asked Rufus, who came and sat at his feet. The familiar meowed and flicked his tail. "I'm guessing that's a no," Thomas sighed. "These girls are going to be the death of me."

Evelyn's hands and shoulders were on fire from strangling the broom handle. She quickly realized that the broom was incredibly responsive. If she leaned back, the broom would jettison skyward, threatening to launch her off the back of the broom. Leaning forward she plummeted toward the giant oak trees whose branches hungrily reached for her. Once the young witch was able to settle her mind, she was able to feel the magic coursing through the broom. With a little concentration, she was able to connect with the magic flowing through it and make it her own. She relaxed her grip on the handle, and let her mind take control. She willed the broom to move faster. In a matter of seconds, she was only a few hundred feet behind her unsuspecting sister.

Night fell like a blanket over the city of Ashen. Brainard flew above the rooftops of a small residential section that lay just beyond the shadows of the Academy. He spotted Gwynevere just in time as she soared by, creating enough tailwind to send him into the canopy of a large maple. "Caw! Watch it!" he called out.

"I don't think she heard you," chuckled Meryl as she traversed along a cobblestone street below. Her eyes followed Gwynevere flying through the night sky until she disappeared from sight. "How curious. Brainard, what resides in that direction?"

"Caw?! Caw?!" Brainard squawked. He was just about to leap from his perch in the tree, when a second broom roared overhead ruffling his feathers. "Caw?! Caw?!" Brainard screeched angrily.

"Evelyn?" gasped Meryl. "What is going on?" She turned her attention back to her familiar. "Brainard?"

The raven pushed off from the limb and took flight once more. "Merry Mansion. *Squawk.* Merry Mansion."

"The mansion… but why would she go out there? Doesn't she know it's been empty for decades." She cast a nervous glance over her shoulder. "What have these girls gotten themselves into?" She looked up at Brainard and gestured for him to follow.

"Caw. Caw," rasped Brainard.

"Yes. Yes, it may be about her vision. We must hurry," said Meryl.

The loyal bird flapped his wings, soaring between the rumpty homes clustered haphazardly together, like a fallen tower of blocks. Below, his master ran through a maze of streets and dodgy alleys. Meryl slid to a stop, and Brainard flew above in a tight circle. Something about the city didn't feel right. The streets were eerily empty for this time of night. A solitary bead of sweat made its way from her hairline, tracing the contours of her flesh, onto her cheek. She recalled the headmaster's words. "Ever since Adelaide's death, things have spiraled downhill. Ashen isn't the same place I once remembered."

The image of the murder victim inside Magdalyn Proctor's cottage flashed before her eyes. The authorities had not only stolen the credit for discovering the body but were incensed that she had been there—even though she was part of the investigation. Was it the fact that she was an elf… or something else? It was well-known that her kind wasn't welcome in Ashen. She made her way down a narrow street and happened upon an old gnome sitting on a bench, beneath a streetlight. Thin ringlets of smoke, rose from his pipe like a halo above his head, only to disappear like a whisper.

"Excuse me," said Meryl softly, not wanting to startle him. The old gnome exhaled slowly, adorning himself with a new ringlet of smoke. "Is there a reason why it's so quiet here?"

"Haven't you heard?" spoke the gnome. His eyes explored Meryl's face, as he puffed his pipe, finally settling on her ears. "Surely you have with those things. What's an elf doing in Old Town?"

Meryl's cheeks flushed red. "I'm here on official Academy business. I just don't know these parts very well."

"I'm sure you don't," the gnome scoffed. "The Academy and the mayor had the place cleared out after the council judge went missing. Wanted to get rid of all the riffraff, so they say. But I'm sure you know all about not being wanted."

Meryl fought back her anger. It was obvious the gnome was egging her on, and she wasn't about to let his petty remarks get the better of her. She needed information, and at the moment, he was her only source.

The gnome pulled a small cloth bag from his pocket, poured the contents into his pipe, and then tamped the tobacco down with a yellowed finger. He patted his pockets and turned to Meryl. "Look at that, no more matches. I'm afraid I'm going to have to—"

Meryl touched her finger to the bowl of the pipe and the tobacco burst into flames. The gnome looked surprised for a moment, shrugged his shoulders and continued smoking. Meryl's eyes watered as a thick cloud of smoke enveloped her.

"Where was I?" coughed the gnome.

"You said that the mayor and the Academy were trying to clear out the riffraff."

"Oh yes," he smiled, pointing a gnarled finger at her. "You would remember that part," snorted the gnome. "No one said that this was the reason, but everyone suspects it's because the judge was murdered, and then they found another body. Another vampire." He shook his head, "And the next thing you know, they've got the whole town on alert. Frightening respectable citizens like me."

"Another murder?" asked Meryl. Was the gnome talking about the body she'd seen in the cellar or was there someone else? Headmaster Ozark had his eyes and ears all throughout Ashen. She would have heard about another body, she was certain.

"Yes, another murder. And…," he smiled sinisterly, "there's even hints of night hunters in town. Purebloods, if you catch my drift."

Meryl studied the old gnome. He seemed to be incredibly informed. "Who told you that?"

"None of your business." He batted her question away with a wave of his hand. "I swear, can't even enjoy a smoke without being interrogated," he moaned. "Thanks for ruining my night, pointy ears."

"Wait," said Meryl, reaching into her vest. She removed a gold ingot. It shone brightly in the flickering candlelight. "If you would, please, what is the quickest way to the Merry mansion."

"The Merry mansion. Interesting." The gnome eyed the gold coin hungrily. He hopped up, and using the side of the bench, tapped the tobacco from his pipe onto the ground. "Continue down this street." He waggled his finger in the direction he wanted her to go. "You'll come to another street that splits off into two alleys. Make sure you take the second alley. Then stay straight for about a mile or so. Trust me, you can't miss it."

Meryl tossed the coin to the gnome who easily snatched it from the air. He pocketed his pay, then before she could ask him any more questions, he hurriedly made his way across the street to a small hovel home festooned between two larger houses.

What an unpleasant odd fellow. Sadly, Meryl was used to this sort of treatment when she came into the city. It was one of the reasons she preferred the forests or even the closed halls of the Academy. Still, she wasn't sure why Headmaster Ozark insisted she investigate this area. She glanced skyward. Brainard was nowhere in sight. *He must have flown ahead to scout out the Merry mansion.*

What she knew about the Merry vampire family history was that at one time, it had been very powerful and influential, owning a large portion of the residential housing. Mayor Wimbly had forcibly seized ownership of most of the properties after an onslaught of complaints from the locals. It seemed that as the vampires' empire spread, so did the attacks. It became a priority when parents complained that their children were waking with bite wounds on their necks.

Now there were two vampires dead, and Gwynevere, a half-vampire, was racing toward the Merry mansion. What had that young dhampir gotten herself into?

A cat cried out into the darkness, and then another. There was something primal in their warnings. There was an angry hiss and then the sound of a body crashing into a trash can. A blood-curdling scream sent chills down Meryl's spine. Suddenly a white cat, its fur stained red, bolted from the alley, a jagged laceration ran from its shoulder to its belly. A tailless black cat hissed and gave chase.

Meryl quickened her step. She cast a quick look over her shoulder, then darted into an empty alley headed in the direction of the mansion. *This is the way the gnome told me to go*. She checked the starless sky for Brainard. "Where are you, you crazy bird?" Meryl whispered under her breath. *Crunch*. Meryl whirled around, her violet eyes glowing in the darkness. She could hear her heart pounding in her ears. Did she see movement? *Brainard, is that you?*

A shadow flickered across the alley and then disappeared. It was as if it had melted into the wall. Something brushed against the nape of Meryl's neck. She spun in a circle, it felt like there were eyes everywhere, watching her. Suddenly, there was a terrified squawking. She threw herself against the wall, edging toward the end of the alley toward the light. "Brainard," she yelled, "in here!"

There was the sound of wings fluttering, a terrified squawk, then Meryl felt a powerful arm around her. She tried to scream, but a hand clamped over her nose and mouth. Her eyes widened in horror as she thrashed about trying to break free. She opened her hands to cast a spell, but the magic spark fizzled out. Blackness creeped in behind her eyes. *What's happening?* Her head lolled to the side as she was dragged into the darkness.

5 - Mansion

"I can see it, Samuel, just over those trees." Gwynevere clutched her hat as she swooped over the forestry just beyond the Old Town of Ashen. Samuel squeaked and shifted around under the brim of her hat. He poked his face out only to reel back from the sight of the ground several hundred feet below. Gwynevere laughed, having never been bothered by the height. "Oh, come on, Samuel, don't be such a scaredy rat."

Even in a state of vegetative overgrowth and disrepair, the majesty of the mansion was apparent. Five towering turrets rose high above the stone walls that surrounded the home. She couldn't believe such a beautiful and grand place could exist so close to Ashen. How was it that her father never found the time to bring her out there? The young dhampir parted her legs for a steady landing in the open field directly under the pale glow of the moon.

"You can come out now, Samuel, we've landed." Samuel popped out from under her hat and crawled down Gwynevere's arm to her open palm, squeaking all the way. "What do you mean where did I learn to land? That, my furry friend, was a textbook landing. I don't see you piloting a broom."

Samuel shook his head and twitched his whiskers. He stood on his hind legs and pointed at the house, releasing another long series of squeaks. "You're right, it is a lot larger than Father's painting made it out to be. I'm surprised you remembered that because I didn't."

A look of pride swept Samuel's face. He squeaked proudly, and puffed up his tiny furry chest, accepting the adulation.

"Yes. Yes, I know you pay more attention to the little things. Perhaps it's because you're little," laughed Gwynevere, poking him in the belly with her finger. She rested her broom on her shoulder and made her way up the winding path to the granite steps of the magnificent home. She paused at the entranceway and took a slow deep breath. Samuel nipped at her fingers. "Ouch, you little hooligan, I already know to be careful," she whispered to him. She was about to knock on the door, when she noticed a rope with a large knot on the end.

Squeak. Squeak.

"I know I'm supposed to pull it, I'm not stupid." Samuel rolled his eyes and scrambled up her sleeve and settled onto her shoulder, hidden behind a curtain of silver hair. "Here we go." Gwynevere gave the rope a mighty yank. She jumped at the thunderous *gong* resonating from the bell directly above their heads. Samuel held his hands to his ears. *Squeak! Squeak!* "How was I supposed to know it was going to be so loud? Quiet! I hear someone coming."

Samuel scampered up the side of Gwynevere's head, squeaking nonstop. "We are not going to die," she shushed him. "Be quiet!" The furry creature released another tirade of squeaks. "Samuel! If she doesn't kill you, I will!" warned Gwynevere.

There was a loud *thunk* on the other side of the door. Gwynevere envisioned a large bolt lock being slid open. She felt her toes clench in her shoes as she stiffened up like a board. Her eyes zeroed in on four ivory fingers with shimmering black nails as they curved around the edge of the door like legs of a huge spider.

Not more than two hundred feet away, Evelyn hovered on her broom, hidden behind the sweeping branches of a towering knot-wood oak. A mischievous breeze ran its playful fingers through her hair, twisting and twirling it this way and that. "Be careful, little sister," she whispered as she watched her far below. Gwynevere cast a quick glance over her shoulder, then disappeared into the dark doorway.

"Judge Aiden?" Gwynevere gasped, stumbling backward into the door. "But you're—"

"No, my child. I'm not Judge Aiden. She was my twin sister. I'm Elise Merry, your father's cousin."

"Oh," breathed Gwynevere, "I apologize."

"No apology necessary, my dear, you look a little shocked."

"The resemblance is uncanny. Not to say that you are uncanny!" Gwynevere quickly added, "You're quite beautiful, as was she!"

Gwynevere stared wide-eyed at the woman who stood before her. She was an entire head taller, thick black hair—shining like onyx—flowed over her shoulders. She wore a sleeved black dress that split mid-thigh, revealing long powerful legs. She smiled at Gwynevere revealing two razor-sharp fangs behind crimson lips.

Elise's yellow eyes sparkled. "Are you going to be alright, dear?" She gently put her cold hand to Gwynevere's cheek. "Come, let's not stand in this dreadful drafty hallway, you'll catch your death." Gwynevere looked at her uncertainly. "It was a joke, my child. Relax. Don't be so serious. You'll get wrinkles, and then you'll never find a suitor." She arched her pencil-thin eyebrows. "I'm just kidding. This way, dear, follow me. We have much to discuss."

Gwynevere nodded and followed her strange relative. The way she walked reminded her of her father. Her feet appeared to glide across the floor, as if she were floating.

As they progressed through the hallway, candles lit, illuminating their way. Aged black and red wallpaper clung to the wall, curling at the edges. Cobwebs claimed every corner. The young dhampir wrinkled her nose—the pungent smell of neglect and rot was overwhelming. They passed from the hall through a doorway, into another room.

"This is much better," Elise waved her hand in a dramatic flourish.

Gwynevere blinked, *that's a matter of opinion.* "What happened here, Countess? It's been destroyed," she said, for lack of a better word.

Elise eyed the room as if seeing the destruction for the first time. Twisted picture frames with slashed paintings were scattered around the room. Toppled plush chairs, their innards overflowing from gaping tears. Dark red curtains shredded from top to bottom. A beautiful black oak table had been cleaved in two. "Oh this," laughed Elise, "this is what I simply call creative redistribution."

"Someone must really hate furniture." The elder vampire nodded in agreement. "Who would do this? Everything is destroyed, what a terrible waste." She picked up a picture from the floor, the canvas shredded. She knew this picture. She had seen it many years ago. In the painting, her father Adonis and Judge Aiden were holding hands. Gwynevere guessed that they were only seven or eight years old. Her father looked regal, dressed in black, a cape over his shoulders, and Judge Aiden glowed in a beautiful white dress with blood-red buttons. They were both smiling, their fangs just beginning to show. Gwynevere's breath caught in her throat.

Elise watched Gwynevere closely. She gently took the picture from her and leaned it against the wall. "Little one. There's a particular segment of the society that wishes we didn't exist. Our family was once revered here in Ashen. But as the saying goes, it only takes one rotten apple to spoil the bunch." Elise exhaled slowly. "Unfortunately, we had more than a few rotten apples. Unable to control their thirst for blood. Some of our family began attacking the locals."

"Father?" asked Gwynevere, horrified.

"No, never! Your father was noble and just. No, it was mostly the young men, unable to contain their primal urges, their lust for blood. Parents began complaining to the mayor about attacks in the night. Children, their blood being the purest, were waking with fang marks on their necks." The mischievous sparkle in Elise's eyes disappeared as the past swept over her.

"Our family was attacking people?" asked Gwynevere in disbelief. "What the heck? You can't blame the townspeople for being upset. I would be too."

Elise formed her lips into a tight smile. "Yes, I imagine so. But that horrific part of our history was many years ago. But as you can see," she gestured to the ransacked room, "the past is not easily forgotten… or forgiven."

"Is this why I'm here? To learn about my past? Not to repeat the mistakes of my family?" asked Gwynevere.

"No dear, we're here to talk about murder, and of course taking back what's rightfully ours."

"Murder?" Gwynevere studied Elise's face. "Whose murder? Your sister's murder? We already know who's to blame."

"Aren't you a spicy one?" Gwynevere's cheeks reddened at the comment. "No, my sweet girl, I'm talking about the murder that took place at your grandmother's house a couple days ago."

"What?!" Gwynevere shook her head. "There hasn't been talk of any murder. That house is under a magical seal. No one has been there since she was arrested."

"I'm afraid that's where you're wrong," Elise frowned. "You see, someone savagely murdered

Darla Valentin, my beloved cousin, and I plan on finding out who."

Gwynevere's eyes grew wide. "I'm so sorry. How horrible." She looked up at the elder vampire, "No one told me anything about there being another murder. I'm afraid I've done nothing but wasted your time."

"You've done no such thing," replied Elise firmly.

"I don't see what I can do. I thought this was about our family and… well, I don't know what I thought," said Gwynevere, her eyes filled with uncertainty.

"Oh, snap out of it, child. Listen, word has it that you are under the tutelage of Miss Ambrosius—"

"How did—"

Elise silenced her with a finger. "She is the ranger that discovered Darla's body. I need to know what she found, what she saw. Everything," she held Gwynevere's gaze aggressively.

"Alright," nodded Gwynevere. "I'll find out everything I can," she flicked her fangs out of habit.

Elise's expression softened. "I know you will. You know, when we were younger, your father, Adonis and I, we played in this very room. Now it's destroyed. Such a travesty."

6 – Missing

"Caw! Caw! Master needs help!" A badly battered Brainard slammed into a tree branch next to Evelyn's head, nearly upending her.

"Brainard!" Evelyn gasped. "What happened to you?"

Brainard wobbled precariously on the tree branch. Blood dripped from his wing and chest where feathers had been torn from his body. "Caw! Caw! Brainard escaped. Master's in grave danger!" he cried.

Evelyn felt torn. She didn't want to leave her sister, but if Meryl was truly in danger. "Brainard, what happened?"

"Shadow took Master and vanished. Caw! Caw!" He wobbled precariously on the tree branch. "I was attacked! Hurry, Master's in danger!"

Evelyn reached out her hand, and gently helped Brainard onto her broom. She thought for a moment. The only people she knew in Ashen were Headmaster Ozark and Dolly. *Yes, Dolly! She'll know what to do!* She gently pulled Brainard closer to her. "I have a friend at the town hall, she'll be able to help us!" she exclaimed. The raven bobbed its head, then nestled in closer as Evelyn shot across the night sky.

Orange lights glowed in the windows of the town hall building. Evelyn gritted her teeth. She'd gotten the knack of flying; however, landing was a different story. She concentrated, focusing on the magic that ebbed through the broom into her. "Slow. Slow," she whispered. The ground rushed up at her. Brainard abandoned ship, or broom rather, and flew clumsily away. Evelyn's eyes began to glow, but it was too late. She clipped the head of a statue with her heel and was flung head over heels into a decorative shrub. Brainard landed with a heavy thump on her chest.

"Caw. Caw. Master's in trouble."

"Ugh," moaned Evelyn, climbing to her feet. "I know. I know." She plucked her broom from a small sapling—straightened her dress and headed toward the entrance of the town hall. "You never saw that," she huffed as she pushed the door open and stepped inside. Brainard fluttered his wings and alighted upon her shoulder.

"Caw. Young witch is a horrible flyer. Horrible!"

"Hello," Evelyn called out. "I need help. Is anyone here?" Evelyn spotted Dolly at her desk and raced over to her.

"Shh!" Dolly raised her finger to her lips. "The council is in session," she said in a hushed voice.

"What happened to you?" she asked Evelyn, noticing her torn dress. She delicately plucked a small branch from the young witch's hair.

"Hey! Pipe down!" came an angry grunt from a very hairy, gruff-looking man in a city official's outfit. He and his partner scowled as they approached. "Who raised you to barge into a government building with such disregard?"

Evelyn regarded the two men… her father was right. Bullies come in all shapes and sizes and all walks of life. She put her hands on her hips and looked at the officers' nametags, Darius and Brom. "A friend of mine is missing and quite possibly hurt. And to answer your question, it was my *father* who raised me to put *people* before decorum." She arched her eyebrows, meeting their stares with disapproval.

Darius laughed and waved a hairy hand at Dolly. "Back to work, ghoul," he growled. Dolly immediately sat and lowered her head. The massive man took a step toward Evelyn, towering over her. He sniffed the air and cocked a wooly brow at Evelyn. "You smell human. You must be that child Adelaide Proctor abandoned in the human world," he laughed evilly. "Explains a lot."

"You smell disgusting," Evelyn retorted, "so what does that make you?"

The behemoth of a man, leaned over her, his face growing more severe. Evelyn felt her body twitch as her eyes began to glow and her hair rose like flames. Books, lamps, pictures, and desks began to tremble. Busts depicting past leaders slowly turned to face the officers. Both men took pause. Brom reached out and grabbed his partner by the shoulder.

"Take it easy," Brom pleaded. "Forgive my partner, he's been taking on extra shifts, and it's made him a little irritable."

Evelyn stared at the two men, then relaxed her breathing. Slowly, everything returned to normal. "I simply came here for help to find my friend. I'm afraid that she's been abducted. Can you help me or not?"

Dolly found the courage to insert herself once again into the conversation. "Who is it, dear?" she asked as she grabbed up a quill pen.

"Thank you, Dolly. Her name is Merylin Ambrosius. She's a teacher at the Academy. Brainard said she was taken, by… uhm, a shadow."

"A shadow?" coughed Darius, mocking Evelyn. "That's all you got, is that she was taken by a shadow?"

"Caw!" screeched Brainard, "Bells Meade district."

The officers shared a look, then laughed. "No self-respecting wolf is going to help you find a missing elf, no matter *who* they are. Their kind are not welcome in Ashen. The Academy has a lot of nerve employing one."

"That's right," said Brom. "If the mayor knew—"

"He couldn't do anything about it," interrupted Dolly. Darius snarled at her for snapping back. Dolly pulled a document from one of her drawers and held it out to him. "Officer Darius, I do not need to remind you that the Academy is not governed under local Ashen City Law. The current headmaster is the sole governing authority, and by law you are required to help *all* citizens. Even the ones you *don't* like. Lastly, Miss Ambrosius was a part of the Magdalyn Proctor investigation."

"We *never* considered her a part of our team. Never!" Darius snatched the document from Dolly and ripped it in two, letting it fall to his feet. "If the headmaster is the sole governing authority over the Academy, and she's employed by the Academy, send the brat there."

Brainard squawked as he landed on top of Dolly's desk. "Missing in Old Town," he said with a ruffle of feathers. "The headmaster will be displeased!! Caw!! Distress!!"

The irate officer curled his lip in disgust and turned away. "I couldn't care less about the headmaster. I have more important business to attend to," he scoffed.

Brom turned and watched his partner storm off. Evelyn looked at him, exasperated. "Dolly," he said, turning his attention to her. "Please, if you would escort this young lady out of city hall. There is nothing we can do. Perhaps you can think of a better option."

Dolly nodded as Officer Brom returned to his post, guarding the door to the inner chamber. Evelyn watched them in utter disbelief as Dolly came around her desk and patted her gently on the back. "This way, dear," she said softly.

Evelyn felt numb. How could they just sweep Meryl's abduction under the rug like nothing had happened? Was this the true Ashen, where only *some* are deemed worthy of being protected? She turned to Dolly when they reached the door. "How can you let them treat you that way?" Evelyn felt anger welling up inside again.

"It's my job, dear," Dolly smiled wanly, "I don't have a lot of options."

"Ashen is filled with all types of wonderful beings. Why would Darius and Brom express such harsh opinions of Miss Ambrosius?"

Dolly frowned and sighed. "There is a lot that is imperfect about Ashen," she said, a sad look in her eyes. "I wish I could tell you more, but now is not the time."

"I see," said Evelyn. Over Dolly's shoulder, she could see Darius approaching. "You better go, before you get in trouble." She took Dolly's hand in hers. "I know your hands are tied. Please don't be a stranger. My father would love your company. He liked your cooking a lot."

"Oh?" Dolly blushed, a faint trace of life washing over her pale skin. "H-he did?"

Evelyn smiled gently. "Yes ma'am, he did. Thank you for your help. I'll see you soon, okay?"

She waved and hurried out of the building. Dolly stood in the doorway. She touched her lips and breathed out slowly, then gasped. "I felt… a breath of life once more…," she whispered.

"Dolly! Get back to your station!" growled Darius.

"Yes sir," she muttered as she closed the door to the city hall.

7 - Mission

"Why was Darla at my grandmother's house?" Gwynevere shuddered. "It's hard even admitting that she was related to me, she was so evil."

Elise ushered Gwynevere through the hallway toward the door. "Yes, Magdalyn Proctor was an evil woman. From respected head of the Academy to cold-blooded murderer, and what she did to your sister," Elise shook her head, "unfathomable."

"So, why do you want to return to her house? The police have already been there searching for clues," asked Gwynevere as they stepped outside. Elise was just about to answer when Samuel poked his head from beneath Gwynevere's hat and squeaked quietly.

"What in the name of Dracula!" Elise shrieked baring her fangs. Samuel shrieked as well and burrowed back under Gwynevere's hat. She could feel him trembling atop her head. "What was that thing?"

"I'm so sorry, Countess. It's just Samuel, he's my familiar," apologized Gwynevere.

Elise held her hands to her heart and laughed. "It has been a long time since I felt life surge through my veins from fright."

Samuel released a frightened squeak from beneath the safety of the hat. "It's okay, Samuel, she means you no harm. You just scared her," Gwynevere explained.

"I'm not afraid of rats, child," Elise retorted. "I simply don't like them. Please tell your familiar, nothing personal."

Samuel squeaked something that Gwynevere couldn't repeat. "He heard you," she smiled.

A sudden scream and then a horrific collision with a statue caused Gwynevere and Elise to jump. "By the blood of Dracula," Elise cried out, clutching her heart again, "are you trying to kill me?"

"Evelyn!" Gwynevere yelled as she launched off the porch and hurried over to help her sister—who had managed to decapitate a statue and disappear into a thick thatch of forest ferns.

"I never much liked that statue anyways," huffed Elise as she hurried over to help Gwynevere. When she arrived, the only things visible were Evelyn's legs and a decapitated stone head. Gwynevere grabbed her around the ankles and yanked, extracting her from the overzealous ferns.

"Are you okay?" asked Gwynevere, helping her sister to her feet. Brainard fluttered to a low branch just above their heads and shrieked loudly, making Elise jump and flash her fangs for the third time.

"Now this is getting ridiculous!" shouted Elise angrily.

"Caw!" Brainard screeched. "Horrible flyer. Caw. Unstable! Killer of statues!"

"Enough!" Gwynevere shouted at him. Evelyn spat a chunk of suspicious-looking moss from her mouth, and then used her sleeve to wipe her lips. "What are you doing here? You can't fly!"

"Caw. Caw. She tells the truth. Horrible flyer. The worst!"

"Are you okay?" Evelyn's dress was beginning to resemble the forest floor. Gwynevere did her best to brush the dirt and debris from her clothing.

"I'm fine, I'm fine. I just can't land yet. And this broom seems to have a thing for statues."

Gwynevere smiled, "It's a special technique. Don't worry," she smiled affectionately at her sister, "I'll teach you."

"You must be Evelyn Moody," Elise smiled showing her fangs. "I've heard you are a sombre suprismo in the making."

"Caw. Horrible flyer. Killer of statues."

Elise narrowed her yellow eyes and glared at Brainard. "One more word out of you, and I'll be making raven soup for everyone. It's quite delicious."

Brainard shrieked and flew upward several branches. "You do realize I can fly," taunted Elise.

The raven nodded, terrified.

"I apologize, I'm Elise Merry," she surprised Evelyn by leaning in and giving her an affectionate hug.

"It's a pleasure to meet you, ma'am. I'm sorry to barge in like this, Gwynevere, Miss Merry, but Meryl's been abducted, and the police refuse to help."

"Meryl?" asked Elise.

"Merylin Ambrosius," clarified Evelyn.

Elise turned to Gwynevere, "She's the elf that found Darla's body. We must find her! Evelyn, do you know where she was kidnapped?"

"Brainard was there, but he didn't see anything except a shadow. He said something attacked him, and he was lucky to get away with his life."

"Caw. Caw. Attacked me in the sky. Very powerful."

The trio shared a look. Brainard was attacked in the air, then Meryl was abducted by a shadow… things didn't look good.

"Brainard, we need you to take us and show us exactly where the attack took place," Gwynevere requested.

"He can barely fly," said Evelyn, "his wing is badly damaged." Gwynevere looked at her sister as if to say, 'he flew here.' Evelyn read her mind, "He felt that he'd rather attempt to fly here, than ride on the broom with me again."

Gwynevere snorted, "Probably a wise decision. Okay, Evelyn, Brainard, on the broom with me."

"I want to live," cawed Brainard.

"What about Elise?" asked Evelyn.

"Don't worry about me," smiled Elise. She dipped her shoulder and twisted her body. She transformed into a swirling cyclone of tiny black particles that merged together, turning her into a bat.

"Incredible," whispered Evelyn.

"Alright, everyone, hold on tight." Brainard wrapped his talons around the broomstick and nestled his head against Gwynevere's stomach. "Evelyn, bend your legs, on the count of three. Push off as hard as you can."

"Got it!" She wrapped her arms around her sister's waist, bent her legs and readied herself for the count.

"One. Two. Three!" The girls simultaneously kicked off. The broom responded, sending the trio rocketing over the trees. Elise tore through the night sky like a demon, her yellow eyes gleaming.

8 - Old Town

Gwynevere and Evelyn hovered above Old Town. Wisps of smoke arose like ghosts from the rooftops of the houses below. A patchwork of window lights shone brightly—the only sign that people actually resided there. Elise flew up beside the sisters and screeched.

"Caw! Caw!" Brainard replied, "This is the place! Danger!"

Gwynevere leaned ever so slightly forward, piloting the broom to a vacant cobblestone street that cut through a series of ramshackle houses. Elise swooped down beside the two sisters. There was a whooshing sound as she transformed back into her vampire form.

"No wonder she was abducted," said Elise, scouting the area. "There's much dark magic here. Clearly not a place to investigate alone—"

"But she was—"

"Not even for a powerful wizard," snapped Elise. Gwynevere's cheeks burned from the elder vampire's rebuke.

Evelyn scooped up Brainard and put him on her shoulder. "You'll be safe here," she said gently. "We really need someone to take a look at that wing."

"Caw! Master first!"

"Is it always so, dead here?" asked Evelyn.

"Don't know?" shrugged Gwynevere, "I never really came into these parts."

The soft scratch of a match followed by a burst of flame caught everyone's attention. "This used to be a thriving town before your kind preyed on the innocence," said a raspy voice. The orange glow of a pipe illuminated the old gnome's face.

"Where did he come from? I didn't even see him," whispered Gwynevere.

"Where did I come from?" The gnome's voice was filled with disdain. "Where did *you* come from? This is *my* town, *my* street."

"I bet he's fun at social gatherings," whispered Gwynevere.

"Our kind has paid dearly for the crimes of a few. We're not here to cause any trouble," said Elise, making her way toward the gnome.

"Ha! Let me guess," he rasped. "You're here to avenge the death of two of your own."

Elise gasped, "How did you know?"

"Good news spreads quickly," the gnome chuckled. "Word is that there are only a few purebloods left."

Elise curled back her lips and bared her fangs. "I would be careful with what you say," warned Elise.

"What, are you going to follow in the path of your family? Continue their evil ways?" He coughed and rubbed at his nose. "You'll never change. It's in your blood. Evil is always evil."

Evelyn turned to Gwynevere and whispered into her ear. "He has a very powerful and unusual magical presence. We need to be careful."

Elise breathed in deeply, fighting back the desire to crush the gnome into tiny little gnome pieces. Samuel poked his head out from beneath Gwynevere's hat—curiosity finally getting the better of him.

"Ah, looks like you brought me dinner," the gnome smiled, revealing a row of yellowed teeth that looked like corn. Samuel gulped and returned to the safety of Gwynevere's hat.

"Sir, we're not trying to be intrusive, we're simply looking for a friend. She was last seen in this area. She's an elf," said Evelyn delicately. "We're afraid she's in trouble."

"Trouble you say." The strange gnome blew a perfect ring of smoke from his pursed lips. "I see the bird took quite the beating." He jabbed the stem of his pipe at Brainard. "You may want to leave him with me," chuckled the gnome, his eyes twinkling mischievously.

Brainard nestled himself closer to Evelyn. "Caw! Evil man! Evil Man!"

"It's okay," cooed Evelyn, quieting the raven. "Brainard is her familiar. He's the one that told us about the abduction. Please, if there is anything you can tell us, did you see where she went? Anything," she pleaded.

"I suppose if you somehow made it worthwhile to me, I might be able to provide you with some… information," he grinned smugly.

"*Worthwhile*," said Evelyn testily, "I don't even know what you—"

"Allow me." Elise rubbed her fingers together and produced two shiny gold coins. "This should be more than enough pay for any *information* you can provide us," she mocked him. The gnome's eyes stared greedily at the coins, glimmering in the glow of the streetlight. Elise locked eyes with him and pressed the coins into his clammy little hand.

"Other's misfortune is my fortune tonight," he sighed. He pocketed the coins and took a pull from his pipe which clicked against his teeth as he talked. "The elf you are looking for did indeed pass this way. She inquired as to why the streets were so empty and about the Merry mansion."

"What did she ask about the Merry mansion?" inquired Gwynevere. The gnome sniffed the air and stared curiously at the young dhampir.

"That certainly piqued your interest. Strange, you're not a pureblood… but your scent is very familiar." He rubbed his hand along his chin. "Anyways," he continued as if it were an afterthought. "I sent the elf to the Elstair Alley, it's the fastest route into the city proper, and also the *deadliest*," he chuckled to himself.

"Interesting how you were here when Meryl arrived, and now, you just *happen* to be here when we arrive," said Elise, her voice dripping with suspicion.

The gnome's eyes narrowed. "Is it now? Tell me, *Countess*, do you know what it's like to live in fear for decades because of your kind? No," he spat, "of course you don't."

Samuel peeked out from beneath Gwynevere's hat. He pulled the young witch's silvery hair around him like a protective cloak as he sat on her shoulder and listened.

"This neighborhood is protected by magical wards. We know each and every being that enters this neighborhood. Even as I speak, you are being watched by dozens of eyes."

"That's creepy," whispered Gwynevere. Samuel nodded in agreement.

"Consider me a protector of the tattered remnants remaining of our lives." He spat at Elise's feet and pointed to a run-down, shack of a house. "And as an *added* bonus, my wife drives me absolutely insane. No smoking in the house, you'll burn the neighborhood down."

Gwynevere surreptitiously eyed the neighborhood. The gnome's wife was right. One errant match would spell disaster, the houses were nothing but old dry wood and nails.

"Thank you kindly, sir, for your time," said Evelyn. "Have a nice evening."

"I'll have a nice evening when you and your ilk leave me alone to enjoy my pipe," he waved them away and turned his back to them. As they turned to leave, another ringlet of smoke encircled his head. He caught Gwynevere's eye as she passed by, her breath caught in her throat. For a brief moment, she sensed a very familiar magic. A tiny smile played at the corner of the gnome's mouth as he turned his attention back to his pipe. Gwynevere's heart beat heavy in her chest as they hurried off to Elstair Alley.

9 – Clues

"That's a lot of blood," said Gwynevere grimly. Evelyn rolled her hands in a circular motion, maneuvering a ball of bluish white light, illuminating the area where Gwynevere knelt.

"It's not Miss Ambrosius's," observed Elise. She pointed with the toe of her boot to ruby-red paw prints leading away from the puddle of blood.

"How can you be so sure? A cat could have run through it," replied Gwynevere.

Elise smiled, "My dear, the blood has a bitter tang, it's neither human nor elf. Human blood is a wonderful sweet and salty mix."

"And you would know because…?" asked Evelyn.

"I read a lot," Elise sniffed. "I am an educated, cultured woman. Every self-respecting vampire knows the pallet of different blood types. This, I assure you, is feline, and dreadful at that, obviously surviving on a subpar diet."

"Brainard, do you remember any of this?" asked Gwynevere, gesturing toward the alley.

"Caw! Caw! Attacked before alley."

"Meryl was attacked before the alley?" asked Evelyn, confused.

"Caw. Brainard attacked before alley."

"So, you saw nothing?" she asked.

"Attacked before alley," squawked Brainard.

"Okay, so you said!" exclaimed Gwynevere. Samuel peeked his tiny nose from beneath her hat. He scurried down her sleeve and into her hand.

Squeak. Squeak.

"No, Samuel, she doesn't hate you," Gwynevere cast a subtle glance Elise's way. "She simply doesn't like you."

Samuel released a lackluster. *Squeak. Squeak.*

"I know you're refined and find it offensive but give her some time, and maybe she'll warm up to you."

"Not a chance," said Elise. "I've killed more rats than there are trees in the Ashen Forest."

"You bit rats?" asked Evelyn, mortified by the thought.

"No." Elise made a disgusted expression. "I simply snapped their necks," she laughed, making a quick twisting movement with her hands. "No more rats."

"Okay. Okay, there will be no neck snapping or talking about mass extermination of my familiar's extended family," Gwynevere exclaimed. "You would think you would be a bit more sensitive given the current situation."

"I apologize," nodded Elise, "you're correct. But," she warned, "should your furry friend accidentally fall under my feet…," the countess raised a sharp eyebrow, "accidents happen."

"She's just kidding," said Gwynevere as she comforted the cowering rat. "You're a part of our family, she'd never hurt you."

"I'm sorry to interrupt such an important discussion but look. At first, I thought it was a spiderweb, but…," she expanded the glowing orb in her hands, illuminating the skeletal remains of a brick chimney, supported by iron framework. A single bloody hair, dangled listlessly from a broken bolt. Samuel, curious as ever, scrambled down Gwynevere's dress to investigate, making sure he stayed away from Elise's heeled leather boots.

Elise leaned forward and sniffed the hair. "That's elf blood," she said somberly.

Gwynevere looked at her sister. It was true, Meryl had been here. The ground at the base of the fireplace was upturned. There was a shallow furrow where something or someone was dragged across the ground. The girls had hoped that Brainard was mistaken, that perhaps their teacher was out on a secret mission for the Academy—that perhaps she and Brainard had become separated. But it seemed like this was not the case. Would Meryl end up like Judge Aiden, or Darla?

Samuel began squeaking incessantly. He clambered up Gwynevere's leg and leapt into her hand. "What did you find?" she asked as the familiar dropped a small piece of red silk into her palm.

Elise's eyes grew wide. She plucked the cloth from Gwynevere's hand.

"What is it?" asked Gwynevere, confused as to why the elder vampire's face had suddenly gone as pale as the moon.

"No," whispered Elise, "it can't be."

"Are you okay, Countess?" Evelyn asked nervously.

"One of our own," Elise whispered. She slipped the silk remnant into her dress and looked at the girls. "You are to tell no one what we found. No one!" she hissed.

High above, sitting on the crumbling remains of the building sat an observer, hidden in the shadows of the night.

10 – Eden's River

"Do you think they killed her?" asked Evelyn. Brainard dug his talon into the young witch's shoulder. "Hey!" exclaimed Evelyn. Brainard eyed her defiantly.

"Master's not dead! Master's not dead."

"I'm so sorry. That was so insensitive of me." She rubbed Brainard's head. "Please, forgive me." She hoped that someone who knew healing magic would be able to help mend his wing.

"Where would they have taken her?" Gwynevere stared at the ramshackle buildings surrounding them. "Samuel, are you able to pick up a scent?"

Samuel leapt from her hand and scurried over to the upturned earth by the fireplace. He sniffed the ground, then began to squeak loudly. *This way!* he squeaked.

"He's picked up her scent," Gwynevere said to the others. The trio dashed off after the rat as he raced down the alley, occasionally stopping to sniff the air, his tiny nose twitching. Samuel came to a stop at the edge of the road. He stood on his hind legs and sniffed the air.

He led them across the cobblestone road, through a small cluster of trees, to a large body of shimmering water. "Eden's Cove," said Gwynevere. Samuel scampered through the grass, to a shallow rocky ravine. A lone post stood in the shallows, a rope attached to the wooden post, moved like a serpent in the current.

Samuel wheeled around. *Squeak! Squeak!* He tilted his head toward the water. Gwynevere didn't need to explain, they already knew.

"How big is this river?" asked Evelyn.

"Dozens of miles," said Elise.

"We need to get the police involved," insisted Gwynevere. "I know the mayor."

"By the blood of Dracula, child. The *mayor*?" scoffed Elise. "I've known the mayor since he was a pudding-faced little brat running around in his nappies. The man is a fool."

"The countess is right. The police aren't going to help us. I've tried," said Evelyn. "Meryl is an elf… they couldn't care less about what happens to her. And… I hate to say it, but both of you are vampires… you're not exactly on their best friends list right now."

"So, what do we do?" asked Gwynevere in exasperation. "There's a murderer out there who's killing everyone close to us."

Evelyn's eyes flew open wide. "Wait," she panicked. "Do you think my father's okay? Will they go after him?"

"I don't know," Gwynevere answered honestly. "It's only a couple hours till morning. Perhaps you could stay with him, and Evelyn and I can continue searching." She locked eyes with Elise.

"Me? Babysit a human? Hah! That will be the day. Unless…," Elise cocked an eyebrow and smiled mischievously.

Evelyn gave Gwynevere an *are you crazy?* look.

"Or not," replied Gwynevere.

"Alright, children, enough of this foolishness," said Elise, her mannerism suddenly turning serious. "Evelyn, I'm sure your father will be safe. I believe the murderer has their hands full trying to clean up all the loose ends."

"By loose ends you mean Darla and Meryl?" asked Gwynevere.

"I do. Don't you find it odd that all paths seem to lead to Magdalyn Proctor? Darla was… murdered in her home. Meryl had been to her home as well, and now she's been kidnapped."

"Why did Darla go to her house? If we knew the answer to that, then it may help us figure out who killed her or why," said Evelyn. Brainard jerked awake—he'd fallen asleep, resting against the young witch's neck. He ruffled his feathers and immediately regretted it as pain shot through his injured wing. "Easy boy," said Evelyn softly, scratching his head.

"I'm not sure why Darla went there. I was hoping to speak with Meryl," Elise paused for a moment as if considering whether to reveal the next bit of information. "Headmaster Ozark told me she'd had a vision. That she had seen Darla. She was in front of a fireplace, burning something."

"You spoke to the headmaster?" asked Gwynevere.

"Yes. Like the mayor, he and I have a long history," Elise smiled at the shock on the girls' faces.

"And he agreed to let you speak with Meryl?" Gwynevere asked.

"Of course, my child. I lost a dear family member. It would be cruel of him not to help me learn more about her demise."

"So, you and Meryl had different visions," Evelyn pointed out to Gwynevere. "Meryl saw Darla and you saw your father. However, she never went into detail about what she saw."

Gwynevere nodded. "It's a lot to figure out. But right now, we've got to focus on finding Meryl before it's too late."

"I agree." Elise looked out over the shimmering water. "Whoever kidnapped Meryl, took her by boat. That leads me to believe that this entire incident was planned. It was no coincidence that she was told to investigate Old Town and—"

"The gnome told her to take Elstair Alley," Gwynevere whispered.

"Like a rat, she was lured into a trap," Elise smacked her hands together.

Squeak. Squeak.

"I know, Samuel," Gwynevere knelt and scratched behind his ears. She then turned to Elise, "He finds that offensive."

Elise smiled and licked her fangs. "I'm famished, and when I'm famished, I get angry."

Samuel squeaked and scampered to safety behind Gwynevere's boot. "He said he's no longer offended."

"Smart rat," the countess laughed. "He just might make it alive through this adventure."

"I agree with the countess," said Evelyn. "The murderer could have easily killed her in the alley. No one in this neighborhood is going to mourn the loss of an elf, and we know the police couldn't care less."

"Exactly," smiled Elise. "Why go to all the trouble of keeping her alive? The only reason I can think of, is her abductor wanted information from her."

"Wait," said Gwynevere, "what information? As far as I know, the headmaster and us three are the only ones that know what she saw."

"Dolly said Meryl was part of the police investigative team," said Evelyn. "Wouldn't she be obligated to share what she found with the mayor and his men?"

"At this point, we have no idea who is involved. Just that they were powerful enough to overwhelm an adult vampire and a seasoned sorceress," pointed out Elise.

"Even if she didn't share it with the police, there are powerful spells that will make her spill... everything," explained Evelyn.

"Then it's important that we find her immediately. And," Elise held up a long, thin finger. "I think I know where the killer is keeping Miss Ambrosius," she smiled.

"Grandmother's house," Evelyn breathed.

"Correct again," Elise smiled. "Magically sealed and protected by the mayor's best."

11 – The Cottage

"This is amazing!" cried out Evelyn as they flew above Eden's River. Luminescent fish swam through the inky black water, glowing like purple and green diamonds. The river ran like a zipper through the lush, enchanted forest. Buoys, bobbing in the water, were left as markers for local fishermen's ghost crab cages.

"I like to call it, *a broom with a view*," Gwynevere called back over her shoulder.

"That's just horrible," giggled Evelyn. "Don't quit your day job."

Samuel poked his head out momentarily, released a squeak, then disappeared back under Gwynevere's hat.

"What did Samuel say?"

"He agrees with you," Gwynevere sighed. "Little traitor."

Evelyn laughed and scooped Brainard closer to her. "You're not so bad when you're not all squawky." Brainard replied with a raspy caw. "Don't worry, we'll find your master." Evelyn's heart went out to Meryl's familiar. He was badly beaten and exhausted.

"Caw! Caw! Rowboat! Rowboat."

"I see it," said Gwynevere. She leaned to the side, then angled the broom downward toward the small clearing. Ruts where the boat had been pulled ashore were barely visible. High tide had done its job erasing any footprints. One glance inside told them they had found the right boat. A dark puddle of blood had seeped into the thirsty old wood at the back.

"I believe Elise was right," said Gwynevere. She pointed at the trampled vegetation toward the edge of the tree line. "Grandmother's house is at most a mile from here."

Gwynevere shifted her weight forward and pressed down on the tip of the broom handle. As they descended, she could already see Elise standing in front of her grandmother's cottage. Her chest felt tight. Uncomfortable. She wasn't sure how she felt about returning to this dismal place so soon. She hovered in the air, waiting for Elise's signal that it was safe to land.

Magdalyn Proctor's home squatted like a gargoyle atop a small grove. The front opened to a field filled with autumn flowers and mushrooms. Blue police ribbon stretched around the entirety of the cottage. A decree with the mayor's signature and golden seal hung from the front door, denying entrance to anyone except law enforcement.

"We found the boat!" Gwynevere shouted as she slid to a stop in the slick grass.

Evelyn nodded joining Gwynevere, "There's blood in the boat. We can only assume that it's Meryl's." She stroked Brainard's head, consoling him.

"I checked the windows. From what I could see, the house is empty. Ransacked, but empty, and… I guess this is the mayor's new security barrier," Elise pointed out.

Gwynevere shook her head and hopped onto the porch. The old boards creaked in rebellion. She raised her index finger displaying a razor-sharp nail and turned toward the door. "A little blue ribbon is no match for—"

"I wouldn't if I—" Elise had barely uttered the warning when Gwynevere was blasted through the air some fifteen feet from the porch onto her back. Her dress had blown up around her shoulders, revealing her knee socks and frilly knickers. Her hat spun like a top a few feet away. Samuel crawled from beneath her hat and rolled onto his back, his tiny rat tongue hanging out of the side of his mouth.

"Well, there you go, you've gone and killed yourself," Elise sighed. She turned to Evelyn and shook her head. "The impulsiveness of youth," she tsked.

"Gwynevere, are you okay?" Evelyn cried out.

"Don't," Elise grabbed Evelyn's wrist. "Sometimes you've got to let them touch the kettle to know it's hot."

Gwynevere raised her head and slowly opened her eyes. "Don't touch the pretty ribbon," she moaned, letting her head fall back to the ground. Smoke swirled from her left hand where she'd touched the magical barrier.

"Are you hurt?" Evelyn winced. She tried to pull away from the icy fingers gripping her wrist, but Elise held firm.

"Been worse," Gwynevere coughed, waving her away.

"So unrefined, utterly unrefined," Elise rolled her eyes. "Let that be a lesson to you. Now, back to the important matter at hand." She turned her attention to Evelyn and released her arm. "Do you think you can get us in?"

Evelyn tilted her head to the side and smirked. "Stand back."

The elder vampire did as she was told. Though Evelyn was young, she understood the raw power she possessed. From the stillness of the night, a cool wind began to swirl around the house as the young witch's eyes began to glow.

Brainard squawked and fluttered awkwardly from Evelyn's shoulder to the ground. He waddled over to where Gwynevere sat and disappeared into the folds of her dress. "By all means," said the young dhampir under her breath, "make yourself at home."

Evelyn's hair rose, swirling around her head. The old cottage began to tremble and shake. *Control*. She repeated the mantra, as she felt the magical energy ebbing through her. Thunder rumbled above, deep and menacing. *Control*. She reached her hand forward and ever so lightly touched the blue ribbon with the tips of her fingers. There was a brilliant flash, then the ribbon disintegrated into nothingness. "Ocitlus," whispered Evelyn. The old wooden door obliged—it opened, inviting them in.

Elise's mouth hung open. "By the blood of Dracula, my child. And you can't fly a broom?" Evelyn turned to the elder vampire, her eyes still glowing brilliantly. "Of course," offered the countess, studying the young witch with uncertainty. "Flying a broom is so yesterday."

Gwynevere gathered up her hat and scooped up Samuel. He blinked his eyes and squeaked dramatically. "Sorry about that," she said softly, smoothing out his ruffled fur with her fingers.

Evelyn poked her head through the doorway and listened. The only sound she could hear was the old boards creaking beneath her feet as she moved. She reached out with her mind, searching the interior of the house. "It feels empty," she said softly.

Elise nodded slowly and held a finger to her mouth as she stepped inside. Much like the Merry Mansion, Magdalyn Proctor's home was now in a state of disarray and neglect. There were gaping holes in the wall, overturned tables and cabinets ripped from the walls.

Squeak. Squeak.

"Of course, I remember," replied Gwynevere under her breath.

"What do you remember?" asked Elise. "Spill."

"It's nothing. Just the last time we were here…," a shiver ran down Gwynevere's spine. "My grandmother kidnapped me." Gwynevere's eyes darted around the room as if the old witch was going to suddenly appear.

Evelyn righted a table, and gently set Brainard down. The familiar paced back and forth atop the table, squawking to himself.

Elise nodded, "So I heard. Wicked old broad, wasn't she?"

"Unfortunately," Gwynevere agreed. "And to think, I held her in such high esteem."

"There's no sign of Meryl," said Evelyn as she returned to the main room. "I just checked the living quarters…, or at least what used to be her living quarters. Her mattress and pillows were shredded."

"Alright Samuel, work your magic." Gwynevere held out her hand. Her familiar raced down her arm and leapt from her palm to the floor. He sniffed the air, twitching his tiny nose, then lowered his proboscis to the floor, sniffing like a bloodhound.

"It doesn't make sense. Why go to all the trouble to bring her here to question her?"

"I don't know, maybe they thought no one would search for her here because it's secured with a magical barrier," offered Gwynevere.

"If that were true, wouldn't she still be here? I've already searched the house," said Evelyn.

"Yes," Gwynevere cocked an eyebrow, "but a proper witch's house *always* has a secret room."

Elise's eyes swept across the barren room. She had circled around the house exterior outside, there were no hidden rooms, unless… her eyes alighted on Evelyn. "My dear, I believe your talents are once again, required."

12 – Revelation

The spell percolated inside Evelyn, *Ocitlus Reveliosa*. The moment her mind connected with the spell, the interior of the house was filled with a golden, shimmering magical mist that covered the walls, the ceiling, and the floor.

All eyes followed as the mist coalesced above the fireplace, swirling and pulsating. Suddenly, part of the wall opened, revealing a hidden panel. Elise shot across the room, her feet barely touching the floor.

"It's empty," she said disappointedly.

"It's okay, look!" Gwynevere pointed excitedly to the floor behind them where golden particles swirled about like a dust devil. The floor shuttered—there was a heavy *thunk* as a section of the floor flung open, revealing another secret nook.

Samuel scurried across the floor. His nose twitched as he sniffed around the edge of the opening. He spun toward the others squeaking excitedly.

"He smells Meryl's scent," said Gwynevere excitedly. She knelt beside her familiar, then jerked her head back, repulsed by the smell.

"Miss Ambrosius!" Evelyn called out, joining her sister. "Miss Ambrosius?" They listened intently, but there was no reply.

Gwynevere rubbed her nose with her sleeve and pointed to a wooden ladder attached to the wall. "I'm going down."

"I'm going with you," declared Evelyn. Gwynevere looked at her sister and nodded, both fearing the worst. She scooped up Samuel and placed him on her shoulder.

"I'll stay up here and keep watch. We have no idea if anyone will return, or if we're being watched," Elise added.

"Good idea," agreed Evelyn as she backed down the ladder to join her sister.

Light from the house proper spilled into the entranceway as Gwynevere helped her sister down the ladder. They both pulled the neckline of their dresses up, covering their nose and mouth. The air was heavy, filled with the pungent organic smell of decay and soil. The floor was made of gray stone, the walls a deep red brick. A hazy green pentagram glowed on the wall directly across from the girls.

"Creepy," whispered Gwynevere.

Evelyn nodded her agreement. She held out her hand—a glowing orb of light appeared, hovering above her palm. She turned slowly in a circle examining the room. "There's a blanket, over there."

"I see it," said Gwynevere, hurrying over to investigate. "I think Meryl was here." She bent and picked up a crumpled, black cloth sack. A length of rope slithered from the folds to the floor like a snake, causing Gwynevere to jump backward and hiss, displaying her fangs.

"You okay there?" asked Evelyn softly.

Gwynevere nodded. Her mind instantly raced back to the black hood her grandmother had forced over her head. She drew in a breath, once again feeling the suffocating darkness. Was the old witch somehow responsible for this? She held the cloth to Samuel's nose. Her familiar breathed in deeply and released a sad squeak, confirming what she already knew. The hood had indeed been used on Meryl.

"Poor Meryl," whispered Evelyn, "if only we'd gotten here sooner."

"Maybe she escaped," Gwynevere tried filling her words with the hope she didn't feel. "We don't know."

"Maybe," agreed Evelyn. She paused at the back of the room. Hidden within the darkest of shadows, a dried puddle of blood called out to her.

Above the girls, Elise silently crossed the room to the hidden compartment above the fireplace. She removed a scrap of paper that had been overlooked and slipped it inside her dress. Then, so as to not arouse Brainard's suspicion, she made a show of searching the fireplace for items of interest.

"Evelyn, what is it?" Gwynevere edged closer to her sister, confused as to her behavior, and what she should do.

Evelyn's body began to tremble—she felt faint. There were voices, images flashing in her mind. It was becoming hard to breathe. She felt her hands cover her ears, then suddenly she was upstairs.

A hooded figure, cloaked in black crouched in front of the roaring fireplace. Books—their innards ripped out—lay scattered on the floor. Evelyn took a step closer.

"Hello? Can you hear me?" Evelyn's voice sounded strange, hollow. The hidden compartment above the fireplace was open. Evelyn could see an archaic leather-bound book with gold writing on the cover inside the secret hiding space. The figure snatched the book and flung it into the fire.

"Burn!" screamed a woman's voice. "Burn!"

The hooded figure cast a quick glance over her shoulder, her face filled with fear. Evelyn took a step back and gasped. It was Darla. "Get out!" Evelyn cried.

"Why won't you burn?" Darla thrust her hand into the fire. She screamed in pain as she threw the book to the floor. Tears spilled from her eyes. She flung open the cover of the book, and began ripping out pages, throwing them into the fire. But still, they didn't burn.

Unseen by Darla, a shadow appeared beneath the front door. Evelyn watched horrified as the door began to slowly open. "Darla! Hide!" She took a step toward the vampire but was repelled by an invisible force.

"Darla!" Evelyn screamed. She reached inside, trying to draw from the magical power that lay within her, but the harder she tried, the more she felt as if she were being torn into pieces. Darkness began to creep into the corner of her vision. Her eyelids began to flutter. Tears streamed down her cheeks. Darla clutched the book to her chest, just as a hand grabbed her by the hair and slammed her to the floor.

"Evelyn, please! You're scaring me," Gwynevere cried.

"I'm so sorry…," Evelyn gave her a crooked smile as her body returned to normal. "I didn't mean to scare you."

"How about next time you give me some warning before you go all zombie-like," whispered Gwynevere, overjoyed to see her sister return to normal.

"I'm sorry. I couldn't really control what happened."

"What do you mean?" asked Gwynevere.

"I saw a vision. I saw—"

"Yes, what did you see?" Both sisters jumped—they hadn't heard Elise come into the room. "Tell me everything."

13 – Celestial Quiver

"What do you mean you didn't see the killer?!" Elise hissed through clenched teeth. She slammed a fist onto the table. Brainard gave a terrified screech and flew to Evelyn's shoulder. The trio had returned to the house proper, where Elise continued to berate Evelyn.

"I told you, I tried to use magic to save her," Evelyn explained, "and when I did, everything just went black. I'm sorry," the young witch scrunched up her face, "I couldn't watch her get murdered without trying to help her."

"You were seeing a memory—you *couldn't* help her. You can't turn back time!" Elise's voice trembled. Gwynevere was uncertain if it was anger or grief, perhaps both.

"I'm sorry, I didn't know that if I tried to conjure up magic, it would destroy the vision." Evelyn's head dropped into her hands. She was exhausted and upset. She was so close to seeing Darla's assassin, and she screwed it up.

"Well, that's it," Elise stated, she pushed her chair back from the table and stood. "Whoever killed Darla has the book."

"What is so special about this book?" asked Gwynevere tentatively. "I mean, Darla was trying to burn it." She braced herself, expecting Elise to chastise her.

Elise took a deep breath and made a small nod as if conversing with someone. "Well, I suppose you should know. Darla was looking for a book known as the Celestial Quiver. It contains a magical map of the night sky that would lead you to five locations, each would imbue you with unrivaled magical power."

"Really?" whispered Gwynevere. "Do you think that's what Darla found?"

"I doubt it," laughed Elise, a little too unconvincingly. "I think that the stories about the book are pure rubbish. I think they were created to give us hope that there is something greater than all of us. Much like the human world and their fantastical stories of deities and supernatural beings."

"Why create such a story? I don't see how it could benefit anyone. Hardly something that would be worth passing on from generation to generation." said Evelyn.

"I can think of a couple reasons. Power, for example. There are those who are always seeking more power. You can imagine how valuable this book would be to a person consumed by it."

"Like Grandma," said Gwynevere. "She tried to destroy our lives just to get what she wanted."

"Yes, exactly. The truth is, there is no such power. Think of your teacher Miss Ambrosius—a direct descendant of history's greatest wizard of all time. She was felled like a sapling. Don't get me wrong, there are hints of immeasurable magic here and there, but prodigies like you appear once a millennial."

"Thank you," whispered Gwynevere.

"I was talking about your sister," Elise rolled her eyes and whispered something about the blood of Dracula.

"I'm confused. A few moments ago, you said that whoever killed Darla has the book, and then you said it didn't actually exist. What am I missing?" asked Evelyn.

"Yes, I don't believe that the Celestial Quiver is a map that leads you to a bunch of magical places and you suddenly become immortal. I believe it actually contains the location of the five sacred artifacts—"

"Five sacred artifacts, now those I've heard about!" exclaimed Gwynevere.

"Yes. At one time, they were hidden throughout Ashen. Each artifact was exceptionally powerful. For example, the ash remains of *Etharius* are said to be able to turn back time. The *Sanguines Drop*, can bring a person back from the dead."

"The book contains the whereabouts of the Sanguines Drop?" Gwynevere gasped.

"I'm just telling you what I believe to be true," Elise explained.

"How did the book end up hidden here?" asked Evelyn.

"Again, this is information that I have gathered from my sources, it may be true, it may not," Elise smiled. "It is believed that at one time, the Academy had possession of nearly all the magical artifacts. However, when Magdalyn Proctor became the head of the school, it is said that the artifacts vanished."

"And no one was suspicious that the artifacts vanished when she took over the Academy?" asked Evelyn.

"No one knew they had vanished until after she was arrested. Magdalyn was the only person with the key and the knowledge of where the artifacts were hidden."

"Well, if she hid them here, they're gone now," said Evelyn.

"How would Darla even know about the book? Or where it was hidden?" asked Gwynevere. "It certainly wasn't made public knowledge."

"I haven't a clue. Unless…!" Elise's eyes flew open wide, "Magdalyn is imprisoned at the town hall, maybe she told someone. Perhaps used it as a bargaining chip."

"A bargaining chip for what?" Gwynevere turned to her sister, she didn't like the sound of that. "Escape?"

"You're right. There is no way Darla could have known, unless she was told where to look," agreed Evelyn.

"No," Elise shook her head. "I have another idea as to how Darla found out." Both girls stared at the countess with expectation, but none was forthcoming. "I'll explain later. Right now, we need to get to the town hall!"

14 – Trapped

Elise eyed the horizon nervously, the sky, a bruised purple hinted at the arrival of morning. "What are you doing child? Let's go!" she jutted her chin toward the front door of the town hall, "I haven't much time!"

"I'm thinking," Gwynevere replied sharply.

"Think faster, you petulant little monster," grumbled Elise.

"Listen, you two, wait in the great hall," insisted Gwynevere. "Only because it will be more efficient. I know the mayor. My father worked with him."

"She's right," Evelyn agreed, "the guards are not the friendliest of sorts."

"Fine," agreed Elise, waving the girls inside. "You forget I've known the mayor since—"

"We know, since he was a pudding-faced kid. You have to trust me on this, the mayor and I have a special relationship," whispered Gwynevere.

Elise arched her eyebrows, "By the blood of Dracula, young lady."

"Working relationship," Evelyn clarified, "based on mutual respect."

Gwynevere made a face and put her finger to her lips. She slowly opened the doors—the town hall was eerily quiet.

"What is it?" asked Evelyn, taking note of her sister's apprehension.

"Nothing," said Gwynevere, "just a little peculiar. I don't see Dolly."

"I'm sure she's here somewhere."

"Maybe she went home," suggested Elise.

"Dolly is a ghoul. She doesn't have a home." Her words sounded painfully harsh, even though they weren't meant to be. "Stay here."

Elise agreed, seeing the first hints of morning approaching through the windows. She stepped back into the darkness of the doorway.

"Sometimes even the dead need a break," came a familiar voice. The sisters turned to see Officer Darius step out of the shadows from his post. Officer Brom joined him.

"Good morning officers. I'm here to see Mayor Wimbly on a personal matter," said Gwynevere, her voice filled with more confidence than she felt.

"You do?" laughed Officer Darius. "She wants to talk to the mayor," he roared to his partner as if this were the funniest thing he'd ever heard.

Gwynevere took a step back. *Why would it be so unusual for me to speak with the mayor?* A voice inside her head told her to be careful, something wasn't right.

Officer Darius caught sight of Evelyn, "Oh, you," he smirked. He leaned forward and crossed his massive arms. "Tell me, did you ever find your missing friend?"

"Yes," lied Gwynevere. "We did. She's fine, no thanks to you." A look of uncertainty flashed across Darius's face.

He turned to his partner. "They said they found the elf." The weight of the statement fell like a hammer.

"That's great," stumbled Brom. "You're quite the detectives," he scoffed.

"Which is why I need to speak to Mayor Wimbly now. I have important information for him. So, if you would please allow me to pass."

Darius clenched his muscular jaws, he nodded to his partner who circled around behind the girls. "Well, unfortunately for you, that's not going to happen."

"The mayor, he got called away on urgent business at the Academy," smirked Brom.

"That's fine." Gwynevere took a step backward. "We'll just wait in the great hall until he returns. Thank you for your help." She grabbed her sister by the arm and turned to leave, but Brom blocked her path.

"You're not going anywhere," he snarled. Before he could clamp his meaty hand on Evelyn's shoulder, he was slammed to the ground with so much force it shattered the marble floor. Darius leapt backward, growling. Evelyn stepped toward him, her eyes glowing, her hair rising. The werewolf turned and fled.

The sisters and Elise gave chase. Even though the countess had incredible speed, Officer Darius had the advantage of knowing the maze-like layout of the building. It wasn't until they cornered him in a dark hallway that he spun around to face them. He smiled and yanked down on a lever, there was the sound of grating metal followed by a jarring boom as a massive door—lined with thick bars—closed behind them, sealing them in the hall with the werewolf.

"Where are we?" whispered Evelyn. A strange feeling was slowly ebbing through her body. Her eyes explored the hallway. Flames appeared to float in space as they burned atop black candles, hidden in the darkness.

"Death row," replied Gwynevere. "It's where Ashen's most dangerous criminals are imprisoned."

Elise stumbled and fell to her knees. "Hurry, before it's too late."

Evelyn shook her head, "I feel so dizzy." She drew up her hands to her chest, closing them into fists. Her eyes began to glow. The smile fell from

Officer Darius's face. Evelyn thrust her hands forward, a wave of blue light flooded the tunnel, and then the young witch and dhampir crumbled to the ground.

"What happened?" Evelyn's voice was barely audible. "I can barely move."

"You stupid fools. So easy to predict your every move. Your magic won't work here."

He's right, I'm an idiot. Black candles. "You won't get away with this," hissed Gwynevere. "The mayor and the Academy are going to come down on you like a ton of bricks!"

"That's ripe, coming from a half-blood whose father killed her mother. Rumor is," he grinned, revealing a mouth filled with jagged teeth, "that you helped."

"You're disgusting," spat Gwynevere. "Why don't you leave? Haven't you already got what you needed?"

"And lose my newly appointed position as chief investigator? The mayor would be so disappointed."

"What?" Gwynevere stared up at the beastly man towering above her. She couldn't believe what she was hearing.

"Yes, for my exemplary work in the investigation of your mother's death and the unfortunate demise of the foul fanged creature we found looting your grandmother's house. Next week, I'll be in an office next to the mayor's." He reached down, knocked her hat aside and grabbed a fistful of her hair. Gwynevere yelped in pain, as he dragged her across the floor.

Evelyn reached out, barely able to move her arm, torn apart that there was nothing she could do to help her sister.

15 – Explodiamo

Samuel slowly crawled out of Gwynevere's hat. Evelyn watched as he scampered down the hall. *It's no use*, she thought, *we'll be dead by time he got help.* She could hear the scuff of her sister's boots as Darius dragged her into a cell. *No!* she screamed inside her mind, trying to drown out the sounds she knew were soon to come.

Officer Darius released Gwynevere's hair, her head thudded against the stone floor, she cried out in pain as an explosion of stars erupted across her vision. He lifted her by her shoulders and shook her. "Stand," he growled.

Gwynevere wanted to sink her teeth into his neck, to pound her fist on his chest, but it took every ounce of energy to stand. He wheeled her around toward the back of the cell. *What is that?* A large silver basin sat atop a squat table.

"Move," he shoved her toward the back of the cell.

"Are you going to drown me?" Gwynevere cried out.

Samuel leapt from the top of the door at the far end of the hallway onto the metal fixture, holding the first candle. He licked his tiny paw, and then brought it down over the flame, extinguishing the candle.

He jumped, grasped the doorframe, pulled himself up, and scurried along the narrow edge to the other side. He coiled his body and jumped again, just making it to the other candle. As he had done before, he quickly tapped out the candle.

Evelyn felt a slight tingle in her hand. Elise's eyes flickered open. Even though she was too weak to move, the countess was able to understand the reason behind the spark of hope. Samuel.

"I'm not going to drown you," sneered Officer Darius. "I'm merely going to make you my puppet."

"Wait, what?" asked Gwynevere as she fell against the basin, catching herself on the edge.

"I guess it won't do any harm to tell you," the werewolf bragged. "This is the basin of memories— a magical artifact that erases all of your memories. *Everything*. No more memories of your family, your friends, you'll be nothing more than a lump of clay," he leaned in and whispered in her ear. "*My* lump of clay." He grabbed her shoulder and shoved her face into the water.

Samuel tried leaping from the second candle to the third, but the distance was too great. He landed with a painful thud on the stone floor. *If I fall one more time, I'm done for.*

He had just began crawling up the doorway again, when he was plucked away by the nape of his neck, upward toward the candle. "Caw!" rasped Brainard quietly.

Gwynevere's lungs burned, aching for oxygen. She couldn't hold on much longer. She pressed the back of her head upward, but it was no use. Bubbles began to escape the side of her mouth—she could no longer fight the urge to breathe. *Sorry everyone, I couldn't be stronger.*

At that instant, Officer Darius yanked her head out of the basin. Gwynevere collapsed against him gasping for air. "Stand!" he ordered. The young dhampir did as she was told. He twisted her around, her head lolled to the side. "Stand!" He smacked her hard across the face. But Gwynevere barely felt the pain. The werewolf stared into her emotionless eyes, liking what he saw. He pushed her forward, out of the cell, into the hall.

Evelyn slowly turned her head, "Gwynevere." Her heart filled with joy—her sister was still alive.

Officer Darius smiled at the irony of the moment. "You won't be happy that your sister is alive for long." He pointed to Evelyn. "Kill her."

Gwynevere didn't hesitate. In a flash, she straddled her sister, and drove her fangs into her neck.

Why?! Evelyn screamed inside her head. The pain was excruciating, but even more devastating was the betrayal. Gwynevere pulled back slowly from her neck, pausing momentarily at her ear to whisper, "Trust me." Hot tears streamed down her face as she wrapped her hands around Evelyn's neck and squeezed until her sister's chest stopped moving. A solitary tear fell from Evelyn's cheek to the ground.

Gwynevere stood over her sister and turned to Officer Darius. "It's done," she said. Her voice, her face, neither betraying the torturous pain that threatened to cleave her soul in two. What was she to do? Her sister lay motionless at her feet and Elise, an immensely powerful vampire, was incapacitated by the dark magic that surrounded them. He would expect her to kill Elise, and then what?

The smile on the werewolf's face turned to unexpected rage. "Kill them!"

Them? Gwynevere spun where she stood, just in time to see Brainard fling Samuel atop a candle holder. Realizing they'd been discovered, her familiar didn't waste any time. He kicked out with his hind legs, knocking the candle to the floor. Leaving only three remaining.

Officer Darius snarled and raced toward Brainard, who squawked and flew to the ceiling, clutching a candle in his talons. "Come down here, you wretched fowl!"

"Caw! Not a chance!" rasped Brainard. He flung the candle to the floor. Darius screamed in rage as it shattered into pieces at his feet.

"Sorry! Very clumsy, very clumsy," Brainard squawked, taunting Darius.

Gwynevere scooped up Samuel and tossed him up to another candle which he quickly toppled. Darius whirled on her, "What are you doing?!" He raced toward Gwynevere, his eyes filled with fury. Brainard dove, attacking the officer's face and eyes with his powerful beak and talons.

Samuel leapt from the candle into Gwynevere's hands. She spun toward the next candle and was about to launch Samuel when a throaty burst of air escaped Brainard. "What's the matter?" he grinned, seeing the fearful look in her eyes. "He a friend of yours?"

Gwynevere couldn't move. She stood watching Darius, frozen, willing him to have some compassion, where she knew there was none. The werewolf held Brainard over his head like a trophy and then threw him against the wall. The raven fell to the floor with a heavy thud. Gwynevere didn't have time to react, to scream at Darius for such a horrific act of violence. The werewolf leapt across the hallway and slammed her against the wall.

"It's over," Darius snarled. He grabbed Gwynevere by the throat and lifted her. He slowly tightened his grip as she dangled in the air. The young dhampir's eyelids fluttered as she fought to maintain consciousness. Unseen, Samuel climbed up the back of Gwynevere's dress and onto the back of her head. *Samuel, what are you doing? Run! He'll kill you!*

She felt Samuel's tiny feet dig into her scalp and then the tiny rat was flying through the air, toppling the candle from its sconce. The candle crashed to the floor. The flame sputtered for a second, then died in a wisp of smoke. That's when Gwynevere heard the wonderful voice of her sister. "Explodiamo!"

Gwynevere placed her palms on Officer Darius's temple, and as she teetered between consciousness and unconsciousness, she found the power within her. And just as her dear teacher had taught her, she thought the word, *Explodiamo*.

There was an incredible concussive explosion. Blinding smoke filled the hallway. Gwynevere dropped to her knees coughing, tears pouring from her eyes. Samuel squeaked, and leapt onto her knee, then climbed to her shoulder, rubbing his tiny nose on her cheek.

Elise knelt and scooped up Evelyn, who was still too weak to walk. "Brainard," whispered Evelyn. "Don't forget—"

"I know!" coughed Elise. The countess tenderly scooped the raven off the floor and placed him on Evelyn's chest. The young witch closed her eyes, Brainard was still breathing.

"You're one tough bird," whispered Evelyn.

Gwynevere followed behind Elise, dragging a bald, eyebrowless Officer Darius by the arm. She removed a giant key from his belt, inserted it in the lock and twisted. The massive, barred door that had imprisoned them, slowly clanked open. They were safe.

16 – Interrogation

Hands in shackles, the disgraced police officers were marched to an empty jail cell. Gwynevere slammed the door shut and glared at the two men through thick iron bars. Brom looked like he'd been run over by a horse-drawn carriage. Darius would probably never have hair or eyebrows again. Both eyed their captors with pure hatred.

"Where is Miss Ambrosius?" asked Evelyn. Darius snarled at her, cursing under his breath. "I'm going to ask you one more time," she said through clenched teeth.

"Or what?" Darius raged. "You don't have it in you to—"

Evelyn's eyes began to glow, she raised her hand, Darius and Brom flew through the air, slamming their backs against the ceiling. "You'll answer me, or things aren't going to end too well for you." She quickly lowered her hand. The two prisoners screamed as they raced toward the cement floor. Just before impact, Evelyn made a fist.

"Are you crazy?!" screamed Brom. "You could have killed us!"

Evelyn's face remained emotionless. She lifted her hand again. Brom and Darius hit the ceiling with a sickening thud. "One. Two—"

"She's dead!" screamed Darius. "Brom drowned her in the Eden River. There, you have your answer, now put us down."

Evelyn turned her attention to Brom. He shuddered under the intensity of her stare. "Is this true? Did you kill her?"

"No," his voice broke. "She wasn't dead when I left her."

"What?!" screamed Darius. "You told me you killed her." He lashed out at Brom with his powerful legs. "You idiot."

"Enough!" hissed Evelyn. "Brom, this is your *last* chance, before I crush both of you. Where is Miss Ambrosius?"

"She's at Magdalyn Proctor's house. There's a secret room. I figured no one would find her there." Evelyn studied Brom's face. She knew that Meryl had been there, but she was nowhere to be found. "It's the truth," he pleaded.

"She's not there now," said Evelyn. She locked eyes with Brom.

"What?" A mixture of fear and disbelief filled Brom's face. "She *has* to be, she couldn't have escaped." Evelyn waited for more, but he remained silent.

"Why not?" she pushed.

"I restrain people for a living." Brom took in a shaky breath. "Plus, she was too badly injured to escape. But then when you showed up and said you had found her, I wasn't sure what to believe. I couldn't kill her."

"You must have been the one that put up the magical barrier," asked Gwynevere.

"Would you shut up!" screamed Darius. He lashed out at his partner again. Evelyn flicked her hand, sending Darius crashing into the corner of the cell.

"Yes," said Brom. "That's why I thought you had found her. As soon as the barrier was broken, we were alerted."

Brom's story added up. They had found the boat, the black hood, and the rope, in the hidden room. Where was Meryl? If she had escaped, she would have notified Headmaster Ozark. But, Brom had set up the barrier after hiding her there, and the barrier was still intact when they arrived. Unless someone else from law enforcement was involved.

"Evelyn. Evelyn." The young witch became aware of a cold hand on her shoulder. She lowered the officers to the floor and turned to face Elise. "I think—"

"Wait," said Gwynevere, "I just need to say something." Her eyes dropped to the bloody fang marks on Evelyn's neck. "Me first. I—"

"No!" said Elise sharply, pushing Gwynevere back. "This is not the time. We can address your guilt and all the mushy stuff later. I'm on a tight deadline with the sun. And if this hairy beast is telling the truth, then maybe Meryl has returned to the Academy."

Gwynevere welled up with anger. "You're so rude—"

"It's okay," Evelyn smiled, pulling her sister close. "We'll talk later, Elise is right."

"Of course I am," Elise sighed. Gwynevere gave her a look that would melt titanium.

"If Meryl escaped, she'd go straight to the Academy," insisted Evelyn. "Plus, Darius told us that he sent the mayor there."

"You're right as usual," sighed Gwynevere. "Let's go."

"You two go. I'll stay here with the prisoners."

"You're not coming with us?" asked Evelyn.

"It's light outside, dear." Elise patted the young witch's cheek. "I'd be burned to a crisp."

"If only," grumbled Brom.

17 - Skepticism

"Let us in!" Gwynevere yelled. "You would think that the world's most prestigious magical institute would know when someone's at their front door." She pounded her fist against the massive doors. "What do we have to do to get someone's attention? Set the building on fire?"

"Explodiamo comes to mind," replied Evelyn.

"Do you really think that will work?" Gwynevere's eyes glowed bright red at the thought.

Evelyn rolled her eyes and pushed her sister aside. "Here. Hold Brainard." The badly injured bird was swaddled in a pillowcase they'd taken from the prison. Evelyn placed her palms on the doors and closed her eyes. She pursed her lips and blew out a puff of air. There was a horrible wrenching sound, then both doors exploded inward in a cloud of dust.

"You did that with your breath? I see more *mint* in your future." Evelyn shrugged and stepped through the doorway, waving the dust from her face. "I may be wrong," said Gwynevere, surveilling the damaged doorframe. "I think these doors were supposed to open the other way."

"Now they open both ways. Trust me, they'll thank me later," Evelyn smirked.

They had barely taken two steps into the school when Mayor Wimbly and Headmaster Ozark appeared, surrounded by a group of stern-faced men and women dressed in colorful flowing robes.

"What is the meaning of this?" shouted the mayor angrily.

"I… I apologize about the door, sir," said Evelyn, glancing back at the damage over her shoulder. "We have an emergency, and we need you to come to the town hall immediately!"

"I was *just* about to do that, when you saw fit to destroy private property," the mayor said hotly. "Wait," he narrowed his eyes. "How did you know where to find me?"

"Officer Darius said he'd sent you here on an urgent matter," answered Gwynevere.

"Officer Darius?" The mayor's voice rose an octave. "You want me to believe one of my most respected officers played a joke on me? Do you think I'm an idiot?"

"Don't answer that," Gwynevere whispered. "It's a trap!"

"Thank you," she nodded to Gwynevere. "Let me guess," Evelyn said curtly, not appreciating the mayor's attitude. "There was no urgent meeting. No need to answer, the question was rhetorical."

"I will not be spoken to in that manner, young lady. You are on shaky ground!"

"Your mayorship," Gwynevere curtsied. "Darius and Brom sent you here to finish their plan. They killed Darla and kidnapped Miss Ambrosius. They knew we were closing in on them, and they tried to kill us as well."

Mayor Wimbly stormed toward the girls, waggling his finger angrily at them as he walked. "You expect me to believe that you escaped two fully-grown…," the mayor's eyes flew open wide and his voice broke at the sight of the black and blue bruises circling Evelyn's neck, the dried blood that had pooled into the hollow of her collarbone.

"Barely," whispered Gwynevere. The mayor's demeanor changed as he slowly turned to the young dhampir. She watched his eyes as they traveled from her purple and black neck to the scrapes and welts that ran down her arm.

"How can this be? I'm so sorry," he put his massive hands tenderly on their shoulders and turned to the others.

"It's okay," insisted Evelyn. "There are more important issues at hand." She gently took Brainard from Gwynevere and handed him to Headmaster Ozark. "He's badly injured."

"Ryzok," he spun and pointed to a thin wizard, drowning in an oversized purple robe. "Take him to the infirmary immediately." He turned back to the girls. "Is Miss Ambrosius with you?"

"No," replied Evelyn, her heart dropping. "We followed her trail to Magdalyn Proctor's house. But by time we got there, she was gone."

"And you know for certain that she was there?" asked Headmaster Ozark.

"Officer Brom said he'd hidden her there. We found ropes and a bag…. I'm sorry, sir. We know she was there."

"Ezekiel! Tempest!" Two more wizards appeared at Headmaster Ozark's side. "Go to Magdalyn Proctor's home. See if you can find any magical traces as to what happened to Miss Ambrosius."

Gwynevere searched the crowd that stood around Headmaster Ozark, her heart sank. "Mayor Wimbly, is Dolly here?"

"No," the mayor's face dropped. "Was she not at the town hall?"

"We didn't see her anywhere—we'd hoped she was with you," Gwynevere looked at Evelyn. "If they've hurt Dolly," she curled her fingers into fists.

"Hurry," Mayor Wimbly ordered, "to the town hall!"

18 – Betrayal

Gwynevere and Evelyn darted through the maze of hallways, down the stairs, to the jail cells. The mayor, headmaster and a phalanx of officers hurried behind them. The booming sound of metal doors slamming, and the slapping of heels echoed off the walls. Gwynevere shoved open a heavy metal door simply labeled Cell Block 4.

"Isn't this the right place?" she asked Evelyn as the crowd of officers spilled in behind her. Evelyn nodded, and pointed to a smear of blood and fur, just outside the door of the cell.

"What is it?" breathed Mayor Wimbly, pushing his way between the two girls. His eyes dropped to the smear of blood on the floor. "I don't understand."

"I think I do," said Gwynevere, fearing the worst. She raced through the rows of cells, shouldering through the doors until she reached a hallway designated for Ashen's most dangerous villains. She slid to a stop at the last cell.

"No!" cried Gwynevere, holding her hands to her face. Evelyn rushed to her side and gasped. Officer Darius lay face down in a puddle of blood. Brom was huddled in the corner his arms wrapped around his knees. The basin of memories was gone, so was Elise.

"I didn't do it," Brom cried out. "I didn't do it!" He buried his head between his knees and sobbed.

Evelyn and Gwynevere were speechless as the crowd swarmed around them. Elise had betrayed them, murdered Darius and for some inexplicable reason, spared Brom's life. She had also stolen the basin of memories. None of this made any sense. The only possible explanation would be that she had help. The girls watched the surreal scene play out in front of them.

As soon as the cell door was opened, a police officer rushed to Darius's side. He placed two fingers on his carotid artery. He turned to the mayor and shook his head.

Mayor Wimbly stood over Officer Brom, "What happened here?" he demanded. Brom remained huddled in the corner, whimpering.

"He's soaking wet," said one of the officers.

"Alright everyone, this is a crime scene," stated Mayor Wimbly. "Sergeant, escort everyone out if they're not a part of the investigation unit. Except for you two," he pointed to the girls, "you stay where you are."

While the sergeant expertly cleared the crowd from the hall, the mayor turned his attention back to the traumatized prisoner. He knelt in front of him and placed his hand on his knee. "Brom, can you tell me what happened?" he asked softly.

The man looked up through wet hair and tear-filled eyes. "I don't know, he was like that when I… I don't remember."

"He may be suffering from head trauma," said one of the officers.

Samuel climbed down to Gwynevere's shoulder and squeaked loudly. "I agree," she whispered. "Excuse me, Mayor Wimbly."

"One moment," he replied gruffly, holding up a finger. Gwynevere rolled her eyes as the mayor and an investigator continued to hypothesize as to what had occurred.

"Mayor Wimbly," Gwynevere raised her voice. "I know what happened." The mayor whirled around—his hairy jowls flushed red with anger. He was not used to being spoken to in this manner, especially in front of his subordinates. Gwynevere ignored his look of annoyance and continued. "It's not from head trauma. The reason Brom can't remember anything is because Elise used the basin of memories on him. That's why his head is wet. Officer Darius tried using it on me."

"What in the world of Ashen are you talking about child? There's no basin here." The mayor spread his hands and gestured to the entirety of the cell.

"It *was* here. Darius attempted to use it on me."

"You're telling me a magical basin wiped away his memories?"

"The basin was stolen from the Academy years ago," said a booming voice. Everyone turned to see Headmaster Ozark had suddenly appeared, his purple cape flowing around him.

"Where did he come from?" whispered Evelyn. Gwynevere shrugged, just as confused.

"It was part of the magical artifacts collection. It has the power to erase your memories or restore lost memories if you understand how it works."

"So how did Darius get a hold of it?"

"Magdalyn Proctor's house," answered Evelyn. "She had a secret room. It's where Darla's body was found and where they hid Miss Ambrosius."

"Many of the Academy's magical artifacts were stolen under Magdalyn Proctor's tenure as headmaster. It was believed that she hid many of the stolen items at her home."

"Speaking of my grandmother, where is she being held?"

"I'm afraid I cannot tell you. Suffice it to say, she had nothing to do with this. The cell where she is confined can only be accessed by a handful of men."

"Like Darius?" asked Evelyn, pointing to his missing key ring.

The color drained from the mayor's face. He turned to the sergeant in charge. "Please see about

Mrs. Proctor." The officer hurried out the cell and disappeared down the hall.

"We think that she conspired with Brom and Darius. Her freedom in exchange for the magical artifacts and the Celestial Quiver's book," explained Evelyn. "But it's just a theory."

"The Celestial Quiver?" asked Headmaster Ozark, unable to hide the excitement in his voice. "It's been missing for nearly a century. Its value in the magical world is incalculable."

Mayor Wimbly watched the exchange, his face betrayed his utter confusion. "How do I not know about any of this? Where is the book now?"

"We're not sure," said Evelyn.

"Not sure?!" Headmaster Ozark looked as if his head were about to burst.

"We think Darius and Brom took it from Darla when they killed her. So, they had possession of it. But now that Darius is dead, and Brom has had his memories erased…, the only person that may have it is—"

"Elise," said Gwynevere sadly.

"What if we get Brom's memories back? Then he can tell us what happened," said the mayor excitedly.

"Not without the basin of memories," explained the headmaster, "and even then, it's extremely difficult."

The mayor looked deflated. He shook his head as he tried to organize his thoughts. "So far, we know Darius and Brom killed Darla, and they stole magical artifacts that Magdalyn Proctor had hidden at her house." Gwynevere and Evelyn nodded in unison for him to continue. "They kidnapped Miss Ambrosius, and we still have no idea as to her whereabouts. Then, you two showed up here to report her kidnapping and that's how you found out I was at the Academy." Once again, the girls nodded. "Okay, I'm a bit fuzzy from there. So if you would, fill in the pieces."

"Darius and Brom were acting suspicious when we got here," explained Gwynevere. "When we told them that it was urgent that we speak with you and that we had found Miss Ambrosius—which was actually a lie—they attacked us. Evelyn took Brom out and Darius ran and led us into a trap."

Evelyn pointed to the black candles that lay in pieces, scattered throughout the length of the hall. "Because of the candles, we lost our magical powers."

"Darius dragged me by the hair to the basin and held me underwater for an eternity, then ordered me to kill Evelyn."

"Isn't the basin supposed to erase your memories?"

"Yes, I know," agreed Gwynevere. "Strangely, it had no effect on me. Except it ruined my hair. It's going to take forever to get these knots out."

"Miss Merry," the mayor motioned. "If you would please."

"Yes, sorry. So, I pretended to kill Evelyn," she turned to her sister and mouthed 'sorry,' "while my familiar extinguished the candles. Then I used *Explodiamo* to take down Darius. It's my go-to move," she clarified.

"Of course…," nodded the mayor.

"We left Elise here to guard the prisoners, which in hindsight, wasn't the best idea, and we flew to the Academy to find you."

"And you think that Elise stole the basin, and most likely the book?" inquired Mayor Wimbly.

"We do, but we believe she had help. It's daylight, and she's a vampire. There is no way she could have done all of this on her own."

"I'm sorry for the behavior of my officers, it's inexcusable. And, as far as Elise Merry is concerned," his face darkened, "she is a thief and a murderer, and she will be brought to justice."

The words had no sooner left the mayor's mouth when the *clap, clap, clap* of footsteps could be heard racing down the hallway. The sergeant slid to a stop, sweat pouring down his face. "Sir, it's Magdalyn Proctor. She's escaped."

19 – Answers

Gwynevere examined a magnificent skeleton of a great winged creature. She peered into its mouth, lined with jagged teeth as big as her pinky. Samuel peeked out from beneath the rim of her hat and squeaked. "One bite, and you'd be gone," she teased.

Evelyn—who sat in a monstrously large chair—walked her feet around until she was facing her sister. "Don't listen to her, Samuel, she's jealous of his fangs."

"Ha! Not in the slightest. I would look absolutely dreadful with those massive things." Samuel nodded in agreement.

"You may want to sit back down. Headmaster Ozark told you not to touch anything in his office."

"But look! There are literally shelves filled with *everything, everywhere* you look!"

"Yes, and it all looks extremely fragile and expensive. I'd really feel better if you'd sit down," she pleaded, patting the chair beside her.

"Mother used to say my curiosity was what she admired most about me," said Gwynevere, plopping into a plush plum-colored chair. "This chair is ridiculous," she moaned, swinging her feet. "I can't even touch the floor."

"I told the mayor not to give you too many of those sugar and raisin cookies. You're like a child."

"He kept offering, it's rude not to accept a gift."

"It's rude to fill your pockets and to take advantage." Evelyn gave her a *you know what I mean* look.

"You're worried about cookies when you should be worried about this carpet, it doesn't even match the decor of this room. You'd at least think it should match the drapes."

"It's a mood rug," said a booming voice. "It changes color depending on its owner's emotion."

"Oh," gulped Gwynevere. "It's actually a very lovely rug." She considered her next words carefully as the rug changed from dark green to a cerulean blue. "So, what does blue mean?"

"Most excellent question. Truthfully, I don't know. I seem to have misplaced the manual," Headmaster Ozark smiled as he lowered himself behind a grandiose desk which perfectly accommodated his size and personality. "I believe it either means serenity or curiosity," he arched a bushy eyebrow.

"I was *just* telling Evelyn, that Mom used to say, curiosity was my *best* feature."

"She did, did she?" he smiled, steepling his fingers. "And what do you think your best feature is?" he asked Evelyn.

"Patience," Evelyn answered without missing a beat.

"Excellent answer," the headmaster chuckled.

"I have a question. Well actually, two if I may," said Gwynevere. Samuel crawled onto her shoulder and sat, so he could be a part of the conversation.

"Yes, of course," the headmaster gestured for her to continue.

"Why wasn't my memory erased like Brom's? And why didn't the magical candles have as much of an effect on me as they did on Evelyn and Elise?"

"I thought you might be curious about that." The headmaster removed his glasses and held them in front of him. The bottom of his cape curled upward and wriggled across the lens. He twisted them in his fingers and held his glasses up to the light. "Perfect." He gave a satisfied nod and returned them to the bridge of his nose. "Oh yes, where were we?"

"You were just about to tell me," *Ironically*, thought Gwynevere, "about my memory."

"Oh yes, yes. Remember your vision when you held the remnant?" Gwynevere nodded. "Your mother and father bestowed a very powerful gift upon you. One that protects you more so than others. A gift that has been passed down for generations." He looked at Gwynevere over the top of his glasses, "You know what I'm referring to, don't you?"

"You mean the Sanguines Drop?" Gwynevere asked.

"Yes. You are a walking, talking, breathing magical artifact. The blood that flows through your veins is filled with ancient magic, and the older you grow, and the more you connect with it, the more powerful you'll become."

"But I was told that the Sanguines Drop was a vessel and that it had been used for centuries to restore life."

"That's right. And what is your body?" asked the headmaster.

Gwynevere looked at him and knotted her eyebrows, *what a strange question*. Samuel pulled on her earlobe and squeaked. "Oh," she whispered. "A vessel."

"Exactly. Thank you for the help, Samuel." The familiar bowed and gestured to the headmaster to continue. Not so much with the conversation but praising him. "Your body merely contains all the, shall we say, important things."

"Like a big giant skin sack," smiled Gwynevere.

"Gross," whispered Evelyn.

"That's certainly one way to describe it," laughed the headmaster. "In time, you will understand your father's words, you will understand the vision that you saw. The magic behind the Sanguines Drop is that, with each continuation, each host, it grows stronger and stronger. The blood that flows through your veins is imbued with the magic that has been passed on for more than a millennium. That, my dear child, is why the basin of memories had no effect on you."

Gwynevere leaned back into her chair, lost in thought. If she was the Sanguines Drop, then couldn't she bring her mother back to life? A renewed hope began to swirl inside her. She had so many questions, but now was not the time.

"Headmaster, what about the book, the Celestial Quiver? Why is it so important?"

His steepled fingers slid into clasped hands. The simple gesture reminded Evelyn of a building collapsing. "I, myself, have never seen the book. But I do know the Celestial Quiver contains a series of puzzles, each revealing the location of a Celestial Arrow. Each arrow works much like a witching rod."

"Oh!" Evelyn exclaimed. "Like in the human fables, where they use a magical stick to find gold or treasure."

"Yes, in this case, the celestial arrows lead to magical artifacts. One of which you are already familiar with, the Basin of Memories."

"So, do you think Grandmother was trying to decipher the book? So she could find the magical artifacts? Is that how she found the basin?" inquired Gwynevere.

"As you recall, Magdalyn Proctor used to have a prominent position at this school. The Basin of Memories was in our protective care. It was stolen under our watch."

"You mean, my grandmother stole it," corrected Gwynevere.

Headmaster Ozark nodded. "I'm afraid so. I think there are multiple reasons she wanted the artifacts. The first, was you, Evelyn. You were a threat to her, and she wanted to control you. Your power would one day supersede hers and that frightened her."

"You should try sleeping in the same room with her. Now that's frightening," Gwynevere pointed out.

"The second," he continued, politely ignoring Gwynevere's comment, "was that if she had control of all the artifacts, then her power would come close to rivaling yours. Your grandmother was trying to make sure that she remained in power."

A crisp knock on the door interrupted their discussion. A young teenage girl in black stockings and a forest green shirt entered the room and positioned herself in the doorway. She stood at attention. Her emerald-green eyes focused on a spot at the far side of the room. Gwynevere was immediately impressed with how the young woman carried herself.

"Welcome, Constance," Headmaster Ozark smiled. "This is Evelyn Moody and Gwynevere Merry." Both girls stood from their chairs and nodded their greetings.

"It's a pleasure to meet you both," she returned a polite smile.

Gwynevere couldn't take her eyes off the girl's hair. Parted in the middle—one side the color of pure gold, the other as silver as the blade of the sword that hung above the headmaster's desk. "They're ready for you, sir."

"Thank you, Constance," said the headmaster as he stood. "I'll be right there." He waited for Constance to leave, then turned his attention to the girls. "We'll have to finish our discussion later. We have something important to tend to."

20 – Secret

Headmaster Ozark slowly pushed the door open and motioned for the girls to follow him inside. He paused in the doorway, and they stepped on either side of him. A gray-haired woman in a flowing white robe turned to them and smiled. "Come in," she spoke softly. "Come in."

The room was filled with cabinets and cluttered shelves lined with glass bottles containing colorful liquids. The room reminded Gwynevere of her mother's kitchen—filled with books and potions. A giant flower arrangement sat on a windowsill at the far side of the room. But the most remarkable treasure lay in the middle of the room, wrapped in cottony soft blankets.

"Miss Ambrosius!" cried both girls simultaneously as they rushed to her side. *Miss Ambrosius*, squeaked Samuel excitedly.

"You're okay!" gushed Gwynevere. "You're alive." She leaned forward and gently hugged her. Evelyn waited, then hugged her as well.

"I think so," she smiled.

Evelyn grasped her hand, their teacher looked so frail. Her face was deathly pale, and her cheek and neck were horribly bruised, but she saw an intensity in Meryl's violet eyes that let her know everything would be fine.

"How?" Evelyn asked, looking from Miss Ambrosius to the headmaster.

"Honestly, we don't know," the headmaster shrugged. "We found her here—in the infirmary—unconscious this morning. No one knows how she got here."

Samuel squeaked, looking around the room fearfully. "Oh yes, is Brainard...," Gwynevere paused, afraid to hear the answer.

"He's fine," said Meryl. She gently pulled the covers back. Brainard was asleep, nestled into her side. He looked like a giant bandage. Samuel exhaled a tiny sigh of relief.

"Alright everyone," said the gray-haired woman with an authoritative tone. "She needs her rest."

"We're so happy you're okay," Evelyn smiled tenderly.

Gwynevere bent to pull the blanket up over Miss Ambrosius's shoulders when she felt something being slipped into her hand. She looked up at her teacher, whose eyes were closed and heard the word "*Secret*" whispered into her mind. Under the guise of straightening her hat, she slipped the object underneath.

21 - Home

Rufus bolted from the porch and leapt from the sidewalk into Evelyn's arms. He released a barrage of meows, complaining about Evelyn's behavior and how she could have wound up dead in a ditch somewhere, but soon he was purring and rubbing his head against her neck.

Thomas flew out of the house like a madman, and held both girls in his arms, sobbing uncontrollably.

"Dad! Dad! You're embarrassing me."

"I don't care," he sniffed through the tears. "I'm just so happy you're home."

"I'm happy to see you too, Dad." She wiped his tears from his cheeks with her sleeve. "Please stop crying, Dad," she complained. "You're going to make me cry."

Gwynevere closed her eyes—it seemed like forever since she had been a part of a family. She missed her mother's hugs, her father's awkward affection. She glanced up at the doorway and blinked. A familiar face peered back at her from the doorway.

"Dolly?" squealed Gwynevere. She raced up the stairs and through her arms around the surprised ghoul. "You're okay!"

"Yes, the mayor and his men found me, thanks to you."

Evelyn and her father came into the house arm in arm. Mr. Moody gave Dolly a huge smile—an affectionate twinkle in his eyes. Dolly raised her hand to her chest, another flutter. She felt a strange, but pleasant warmth filling her body.

"Something smells incredible," moaned Gwynevere. "I'm starving."

"Dolly made breakfast," Thomas said happily, "and trust me, it is delicious." He turned to Dolly, a mischievous look in his eye. "I'm sorry, I couldn't help myself."

"You're excused this time," said Dolly sternly, "but from now on, you must practice restraint."

"Yes ma'am," he blushed. Gwynevere and Evelyn gave each other a *what is going on with them* look.

As Thomas and Dolly disappeared into the kitchen, Gwynevere grabbed Evelyn's hand. "Look, I never got to properly apologize for biting you." She looked at the angry bruise on her sister's neck. "Did it hurt horribly?" she felt tears welling up in her eyes.

"It was excruciating," said Evelyn, rubbing her neck. "But you know what hurts worse than your canines? The betrayal."

Gwynevere's lips began to tremble. Betrayal. "I had to. Darius would have killed us all. I had to convince—"

Evelyn held up her index finger, mushing Gwynevere's lips. "I know. I'm just messing with you."

"You're so mean!" laughed Gwynevere, grabbing Evelyn's shoulders and shaking her. "Well, just so you know," she smirked, "you taste horrible."

"Oh, Gwynevere," Evelyn threw her arm around her sister's shoulder, "you're such a mess. A gorgeous mess," she winked, "but still, a mess."

Gwynevere sat alone in her room, staring at the piece of red silk Meryl had pressed into her hand. Tears welled up in her eyes. "Father?"

More from T. Lockhaven

We hope you enjoyed reading *Bittersweet Deceit*, the second book in *Merry and Moody Witch Cozy Mysteries* series. Let us know what you think by leaving a review on Amazon, Barnes & Noble and/or Goodreads. Thank you so very much!

Follow T. Lockhaven's author page on Amazon or on Goodreads for new release updates and giveaways.

<u>Merry and Moody Witch Cozy Mysteries</u>
Book 1: Potion Commotion
Book 2: Bittersweet Deceit

Other cozy mysteries by T. Lockhaven

The Coffee House Sleuths

Book 1: A Garden to Die For
Book 2: A Mummy to Die For
Upcoming: A Role to Die For
Upcoming: A Voyage to Die For

Also written in the series is *Sleighed*, the first book in *The Coffee House Sleuths: A Christmas Cozy Mystery*. *Sleighed* takes place in the same town, with the same characters, but was written as a fun standalone Christmas story.

Thomas Lockhaven

T. Lockhaven is also a children's author under the name Thomas Lockhaven.

Quest Chasers (Ongoing Series)
Book 1: The Deadly Cavern
Book 2: The Screaming Mummy

Ava & Carol Detective Agency (Ongoing Series)
Book 1: The Mystery of the Pharaoh's Diamonds
Book 2: The Mystery of Solomon's Ring
Book 3: The Haunted Mansion
Book 4: Dognapped
Book 5: The Eye of God
Book 6: The Crown Jewels Mystery
Book 7: The Curse of the Red Devil
Book 8: The Witch's Secret
Book 9: The Christmas Thief

Calista Chase Time Sleuth (Ongoing Series)
Book 1: Blackbeard's Treasure

The Ghosts of Ian Stanley (Ongoing Series)

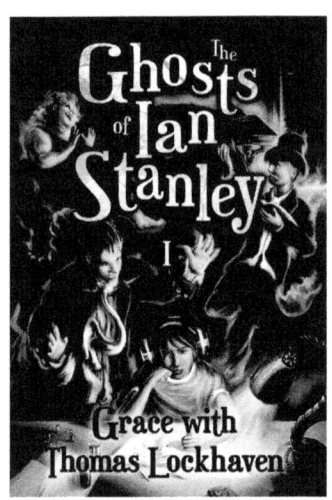

Printed in Great Britain
by Amazon

77599048R00099